MARK TWAIN'S

THE ADVENTURES OF
TOM SAWYER

A GRAPHIC NOVEL

BY M.C. HALL &
DANIEL STRICKLAND

STONE ARCH BOOKS
A CAPSTONE IMPRINT

Graphic Revolve is published by Stone Arch Books
A Capstone Imprint
1710 Roe Crest Drive, North Mankato, Minnesota 56003
www.capstonepub.com

Cataloging-in-Publication Data is available on the Library
of Congress website.
Hardcover ISBN: 978-1-4965-0003-8
Paperback ISBN: 978-1-4965-0022-9

Summary: Tom Sawyer and Huckleberry Finn think they
are clever characters. When Tom and Huck witness a
murder, however, they find themselves hurled into a
series of adventures that lead them to some seriously
frightening situations.

Common Core back matter written by Dr. Katie Monnin.

Designer: Bob Lentz
Assistant Designer: Peggie Carley
Editor: Donald Lemke
Assistant Editor: Sean Tulien
Creative Director: Heather Kindseth
Editorial Director: Michael Dahl
Publisher: Ashley C. Andersen Zantop

Printed in the United States of America.
022019   000066

TABLE OF CONTENTS

ABOUT MARK TWAIN

Mark Twain was born in Hannibal, Missouri in 1835. An adventurous young man, Twain traveled around the United States. He worked as a Mississippi riverboat pilot, a miner, and a reporter. When Twain wrote *The Adventures of Tom Sawyer* in 1872, most other books presented boys as purely good or evil characters. Twain wanted his boy hero, Tom Sawyer, to act like a real boy, so he based the book on his own boyhood adventures in Missouri.

Set sometime between 1830 and 1840, the story shows small-town life along the Mississippi River. At the time of the story, steamboats changed the way people and goods traveled. Before the invention of steamboats, it often took months to travel between the major river ports of New Orleans and Minneapolis. However, steamboats could make this journey in just ten days.

Throughout *The Adventures of Tom Sawyer*, Twain presented the kinds of people he knew from his hometown. Some of these people were important figures in the town, like Judge Thatcher. Others, like Muff Potter, were poor drifters who were drawn to schemes for getting rich. The one character who seems different from the rest is Injun Joe. The word "Injun" is a slang word for "Indian" or "Native American." Mark Twain didn't know much about Native Americans, so he based Injun Joe on stereotypes, or unfair beliefs, that many Americans held during that time.

Tom Sawyer

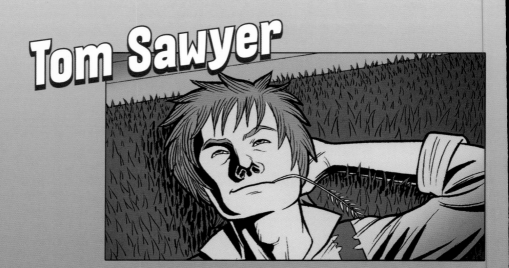

Joe Harper

Huckelberry Finn

Aunt Polly

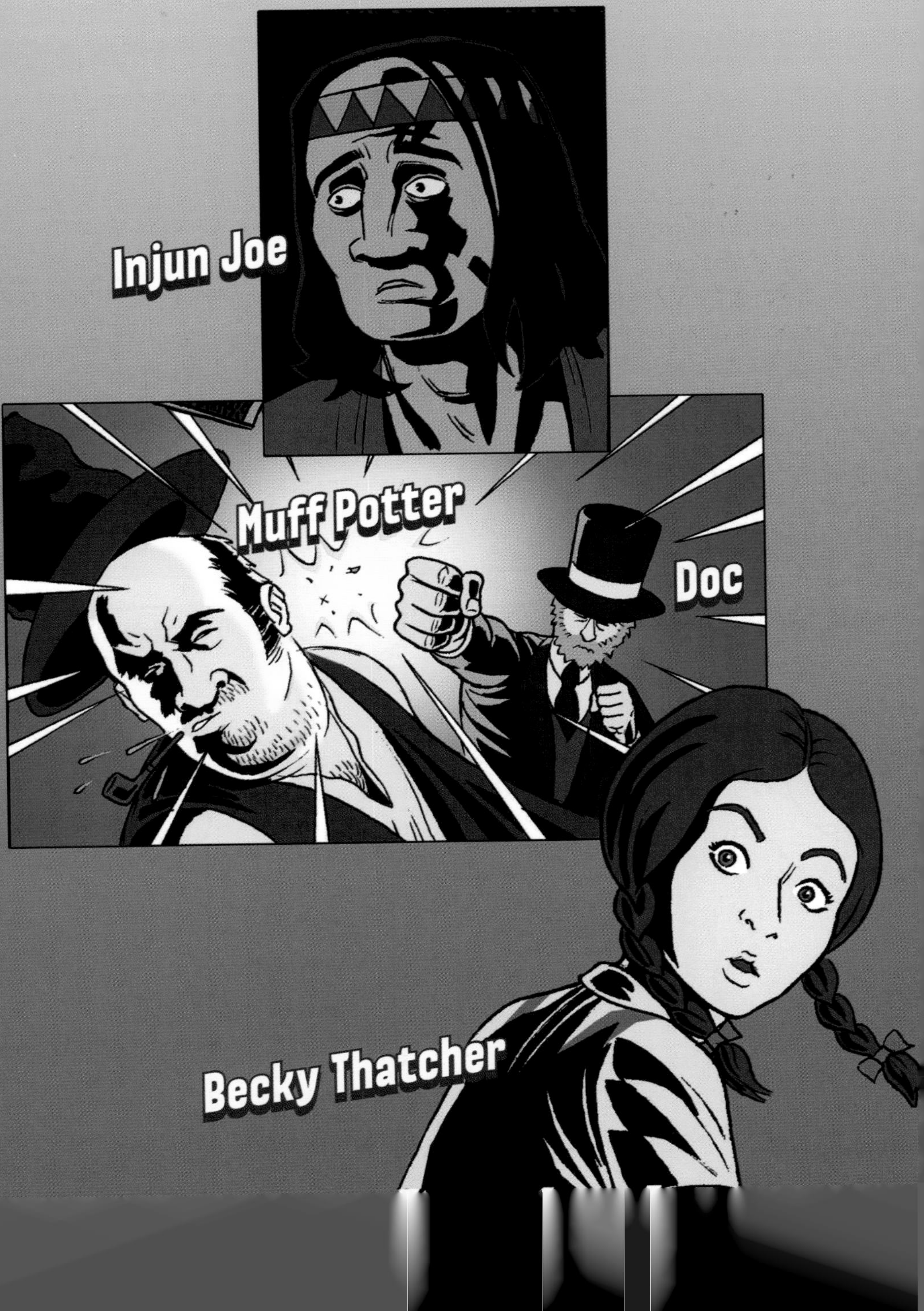
Injun Joe
Muff Potter
Doc
Becky Thatcher

CHAPTER 1
TOM IN TROUBLE

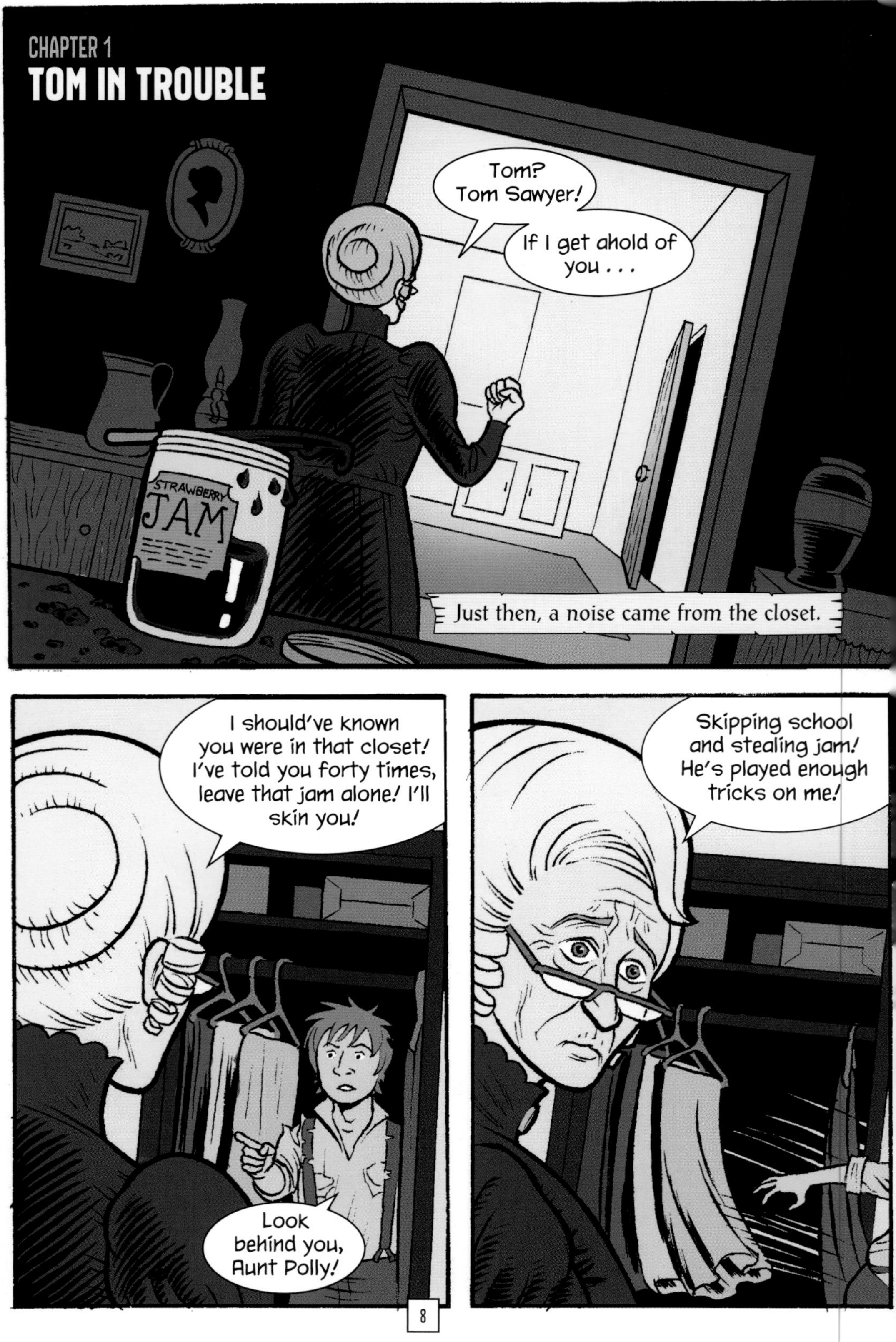

Tom? Tom Sawyer!
If I get ahold of you . . .
Just then, a noise came from the closet.
I should've known you were in that closet! I've told you forty times, leave that jam alone! I'll skin you!
Look behind you, Aunt Polly!
Skipping school and stealing jam! He's played enough tricks on me!
STRAWBERRY JAM

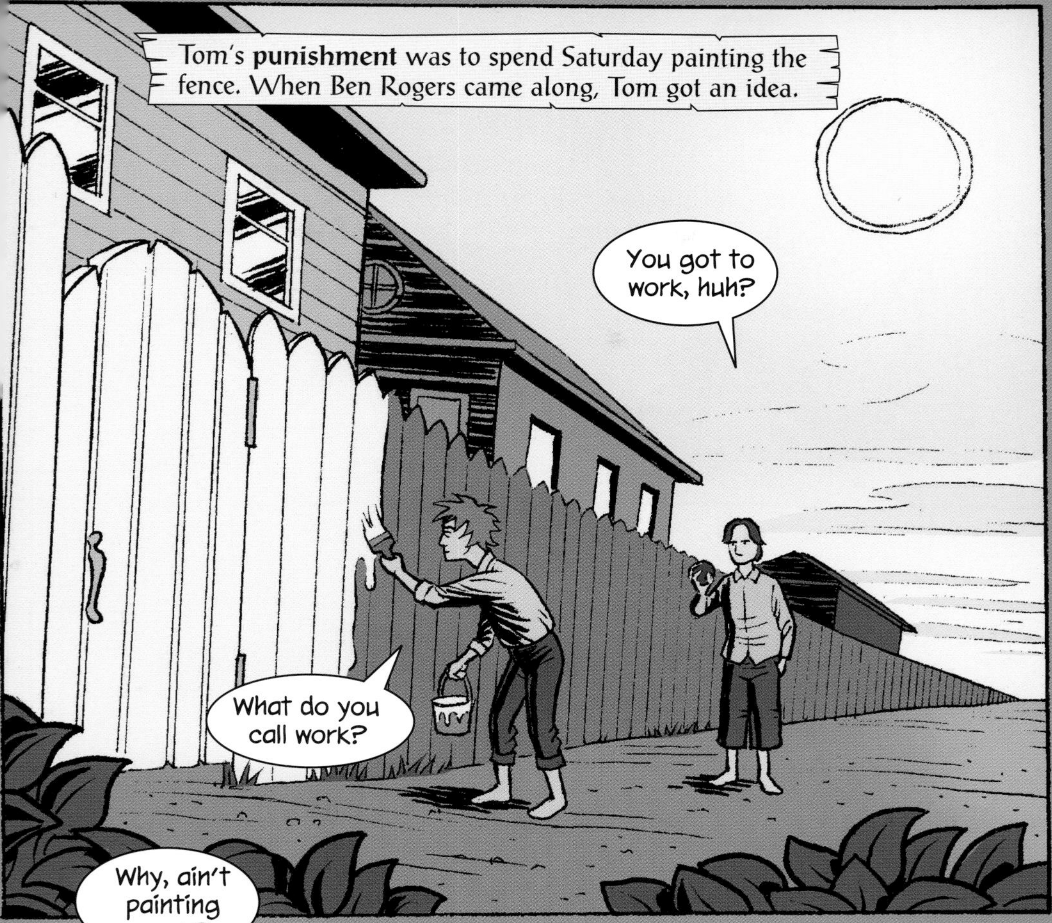
Tom's **punishment** was to spend Saturday painting the fence. When Ben Rogers came along, Tom got an idea.
You got to work, huh?
What do you call work?

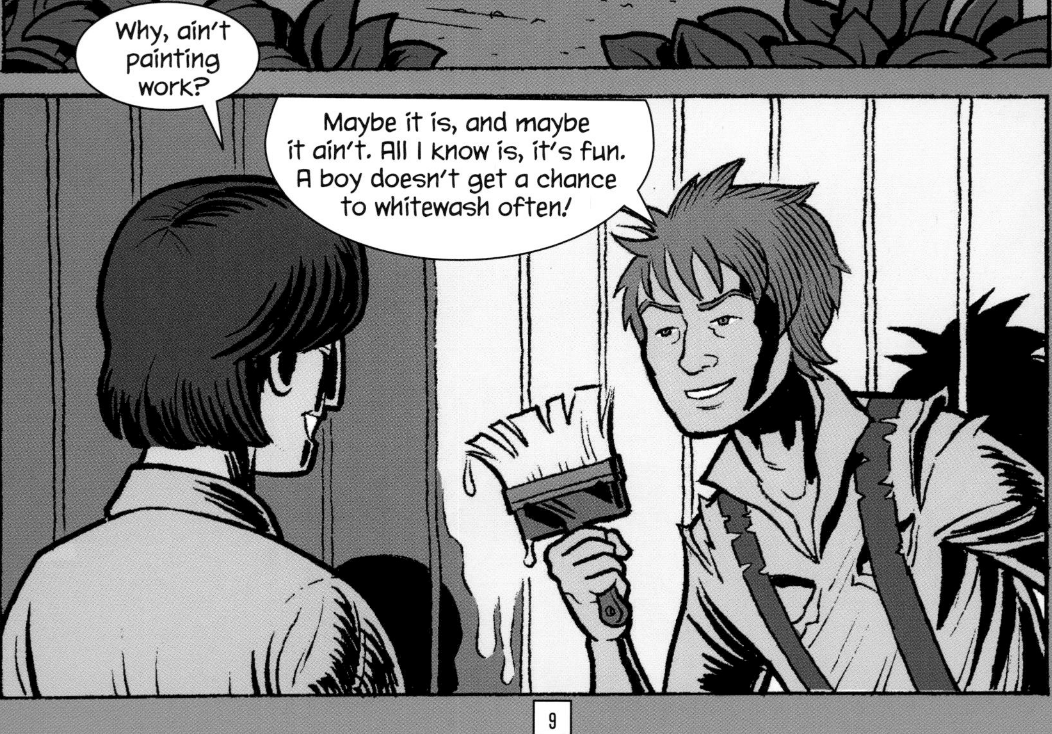
Why, ain't painting work?
Maybe it is, and maybe it ain't. All I know is, it's fun. A boy doesn't get a chance to whitewash often!

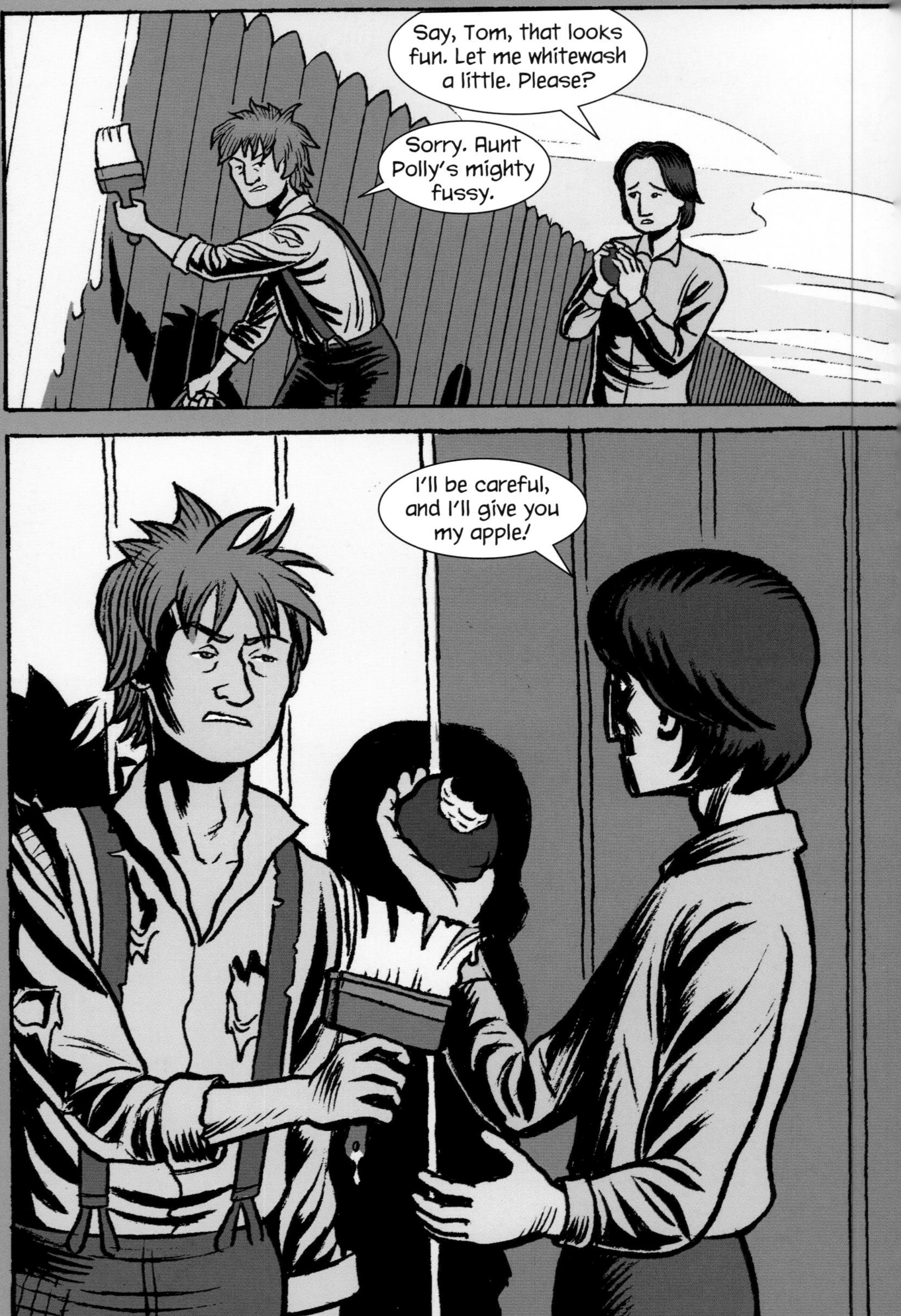
Say, Tom, that looks fun. Let me whitewash a little. Please?
Sorry. Aunt Polly's mighty fussy.
I'll be careful, and I'll give you my apple!

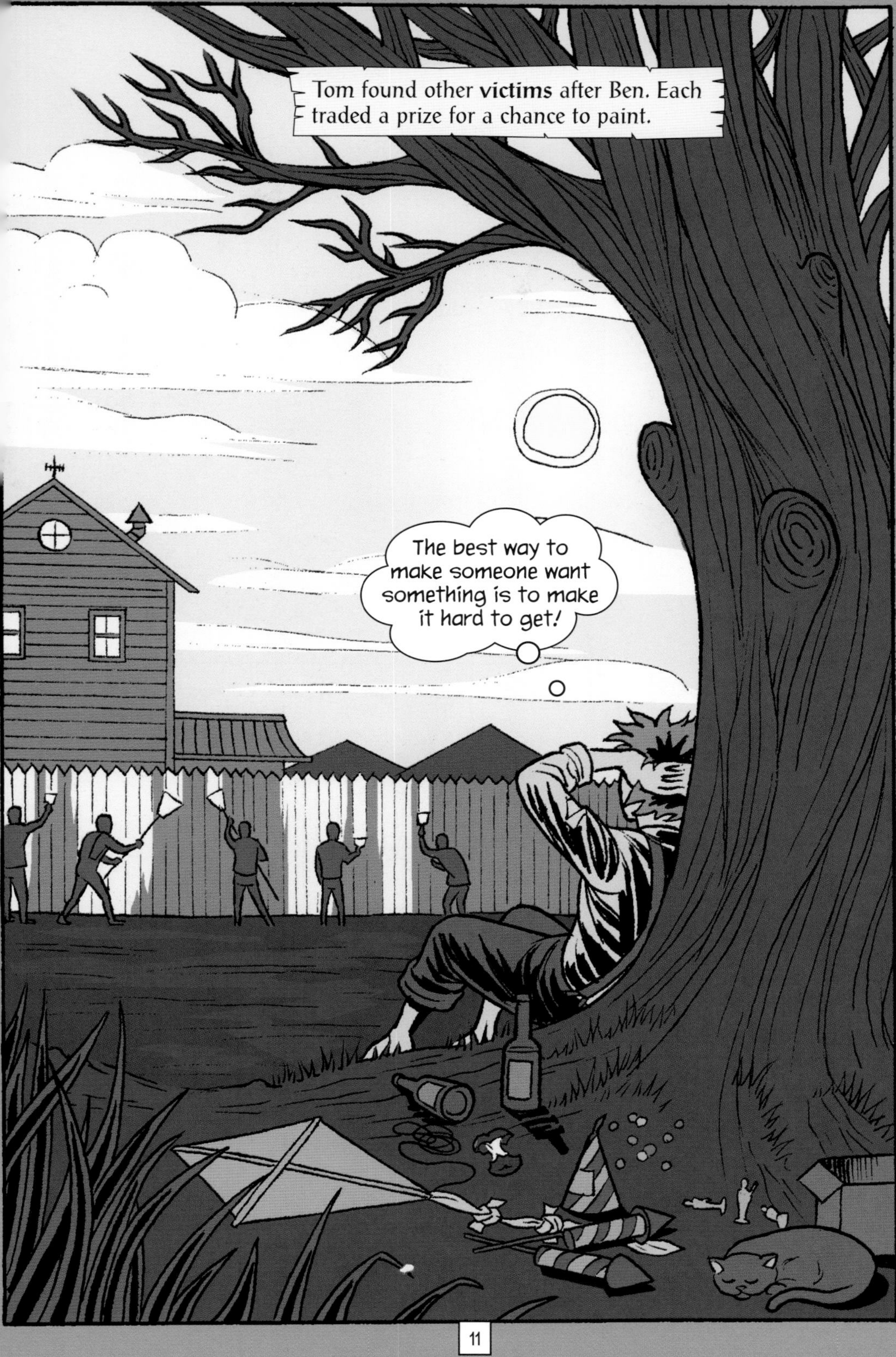
Tom found other **victims** after Ben. Each traded a prize for a chance to paint.
The best way to make someone want something is to make it hard to get!

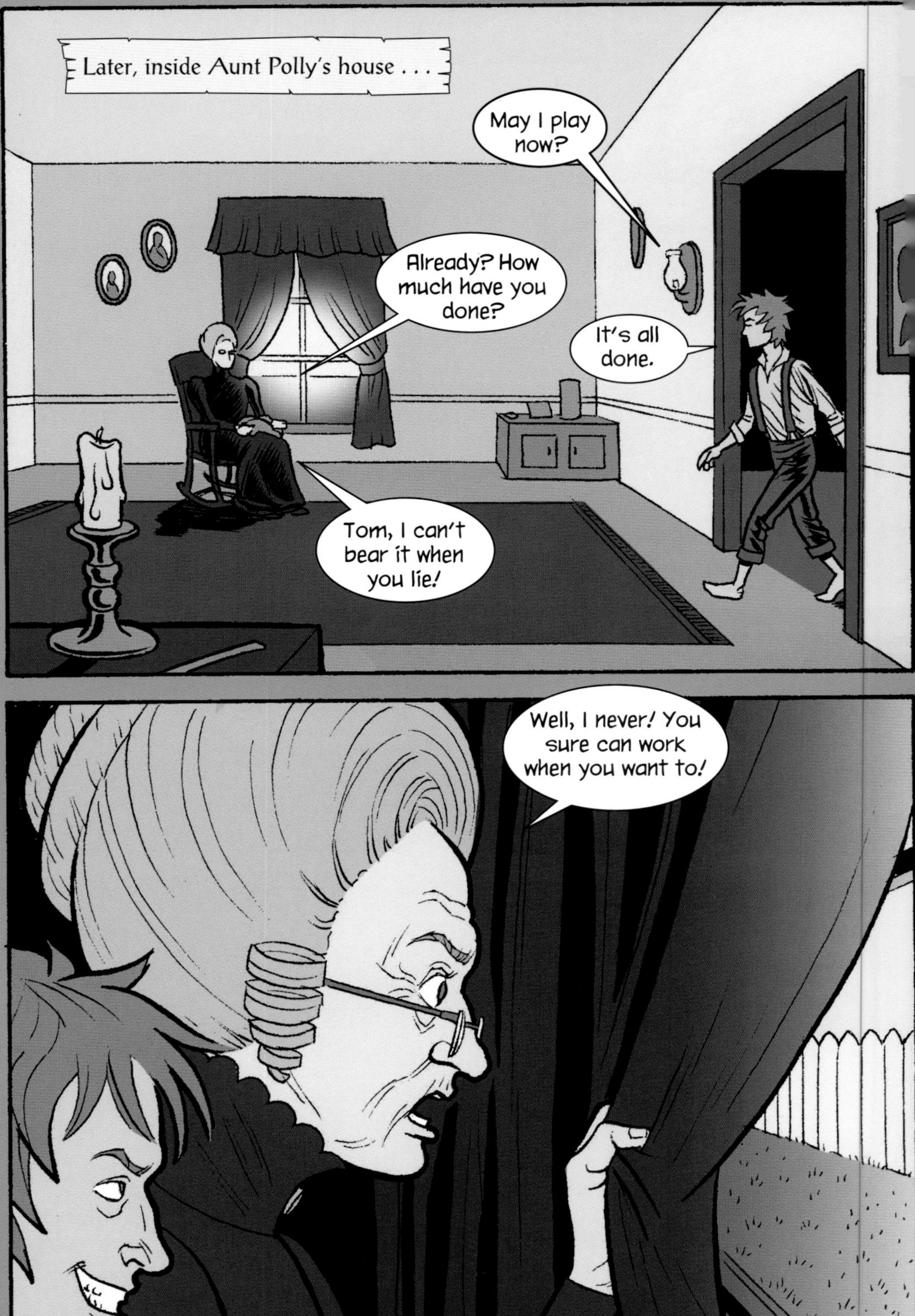
Later, inside Aunt Polly's house . . .
May I play now?
Already? How much have you done?
It's all done.
Tom, I can't bear it when you lie!
Well, I never! You sure can work when you want to!

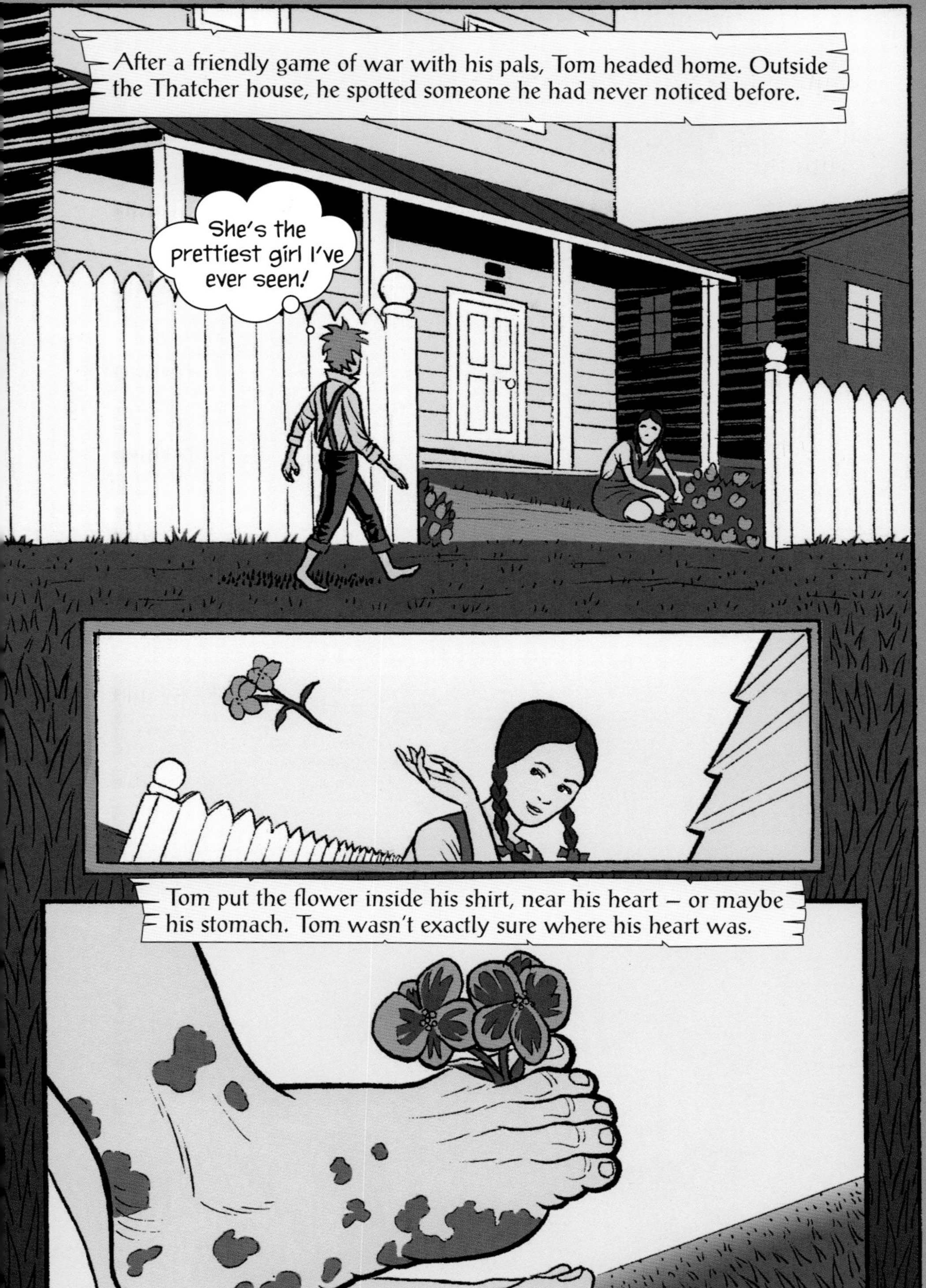
After a friendly game of war with his pals, Tom headed home. Outside the Thatcher house, he spotted someone he had never noticed before.
She's the prettiest girl I've ever seen!
Tom put the flower inside his shirt, near his heart – or maybe his stomach. Tom wasn't exactly sure where his heart was.

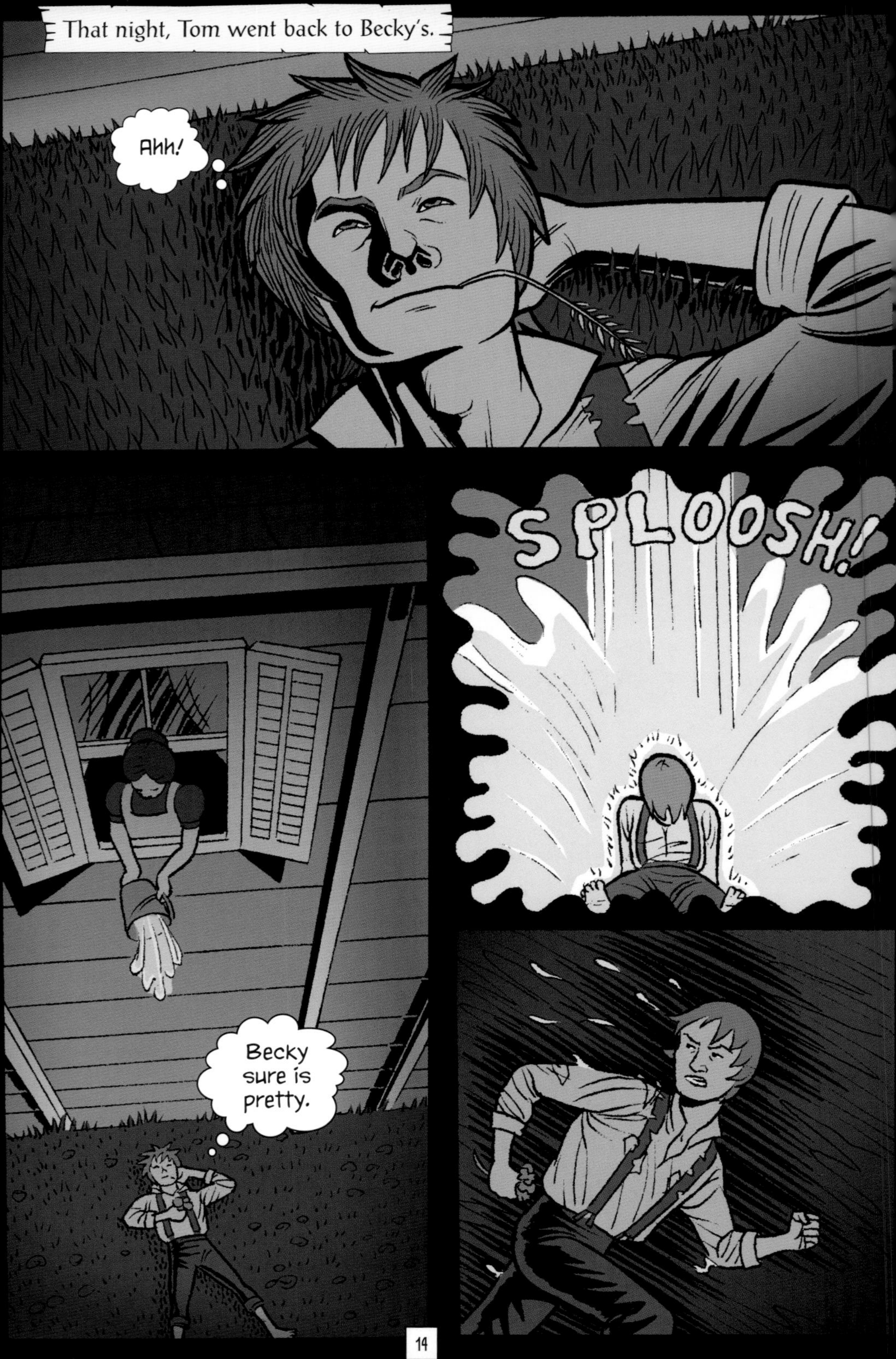
That night, Tom went back to Becky's.
Ahh!
Becky sure is pretty.
SPLOOSH!

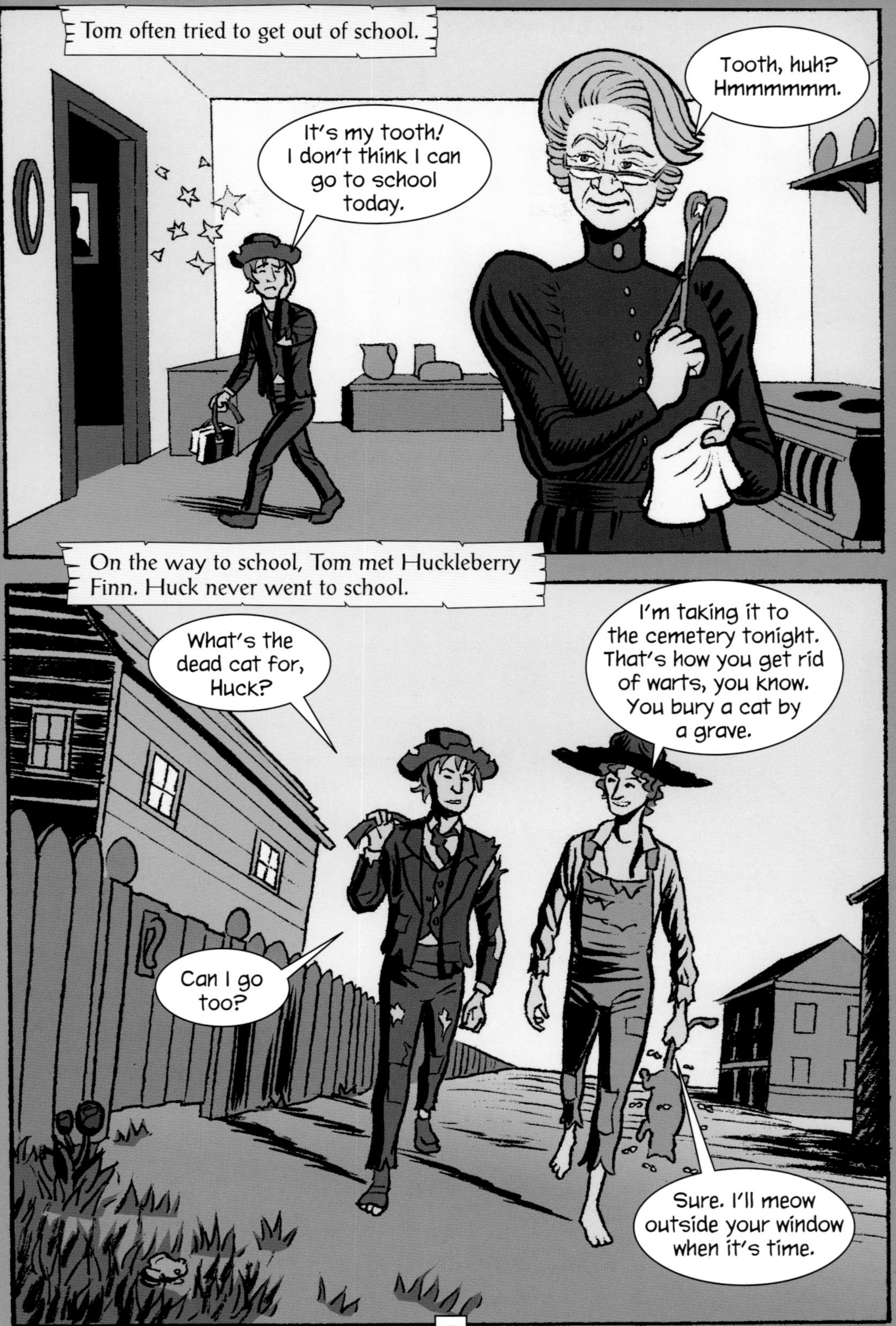
Tom often tried to get out of school.
It's my tooth! I don't think I can go to school today.
Tooth, huh? Hmmmmmm.
On the way to school, Tom met Huckleberry Finn. Huck never went to school.
What's the dead cat for, Huck?
I'm taking it to the cemetery tonight. That's how you get rid of warts, you know. You bury a cat by a grave.
Can I go too?
Sure. I'll meow outside your window when it's time.

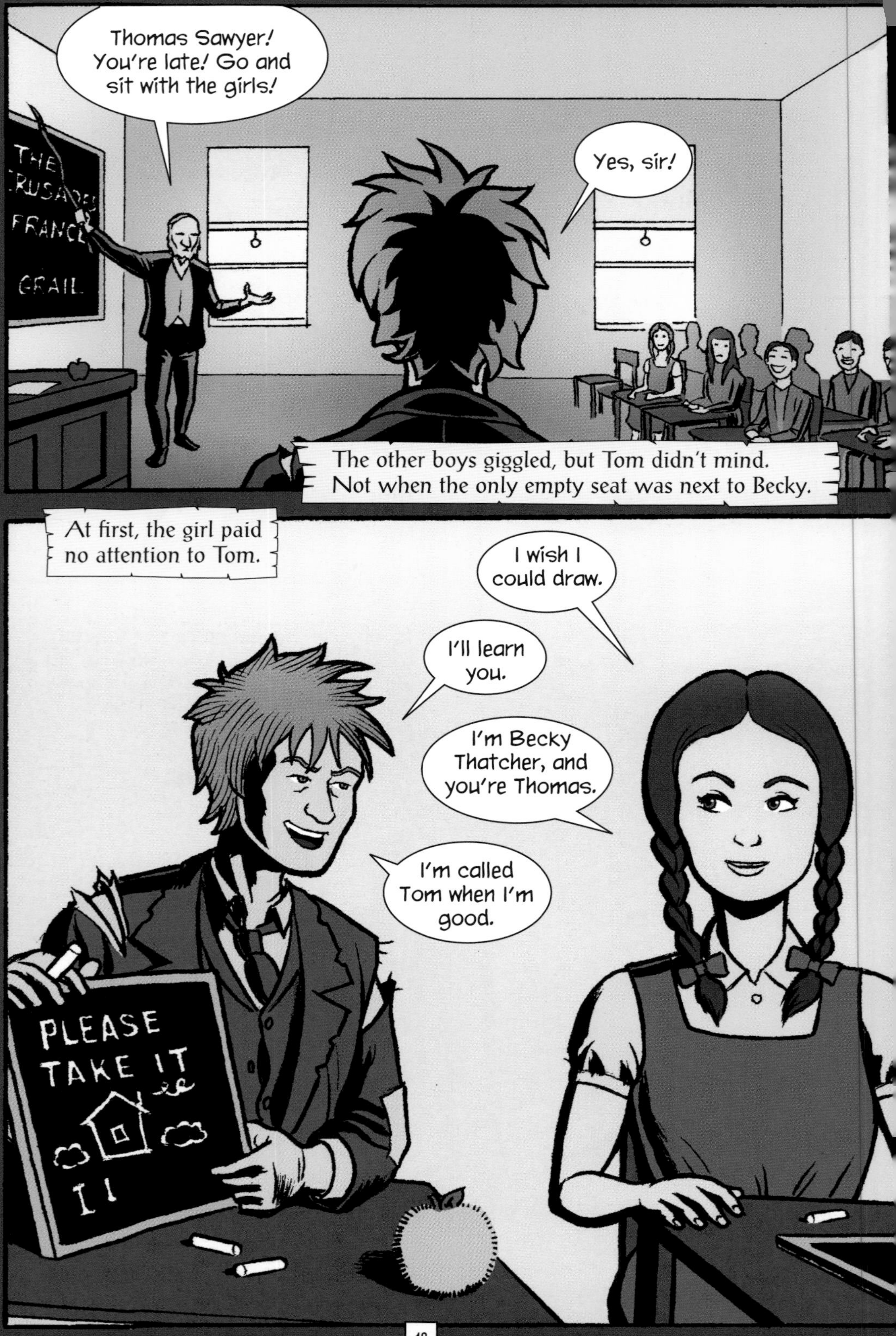
Thomas Sawyer! You're late! Go and sit with the girls!
Yes, sir!
THE CRUSADES FRANCE GRAIL
The other boys giggled, but Tom didn't mind. Not when the only empty seat was next to Becky.
At first, the girl paid no attention to Tom.
I wish I could draw.
I'll learn you.
I'm Becky Thatcher, and you're Thomas.
I'm called Tom when I'm good.
PLEASE TAKE IT

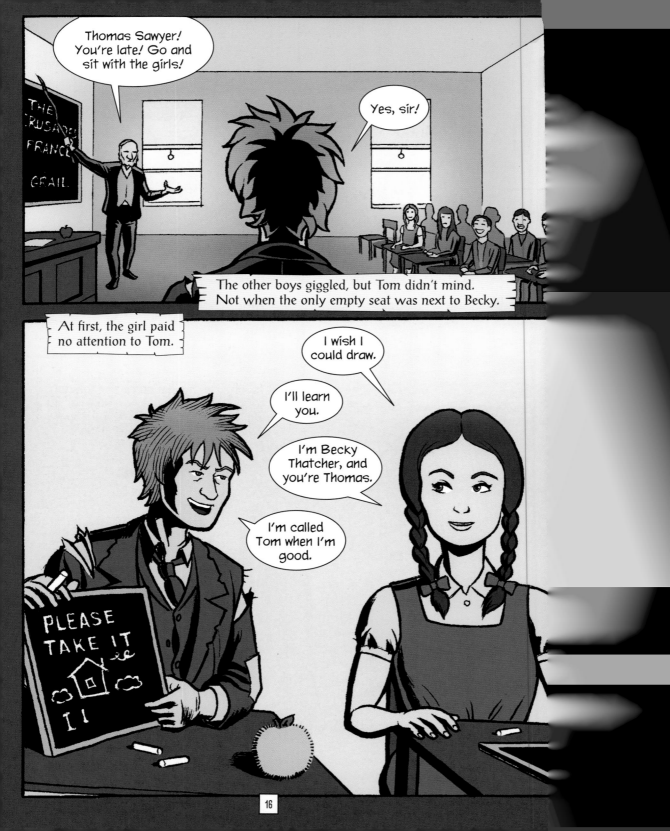

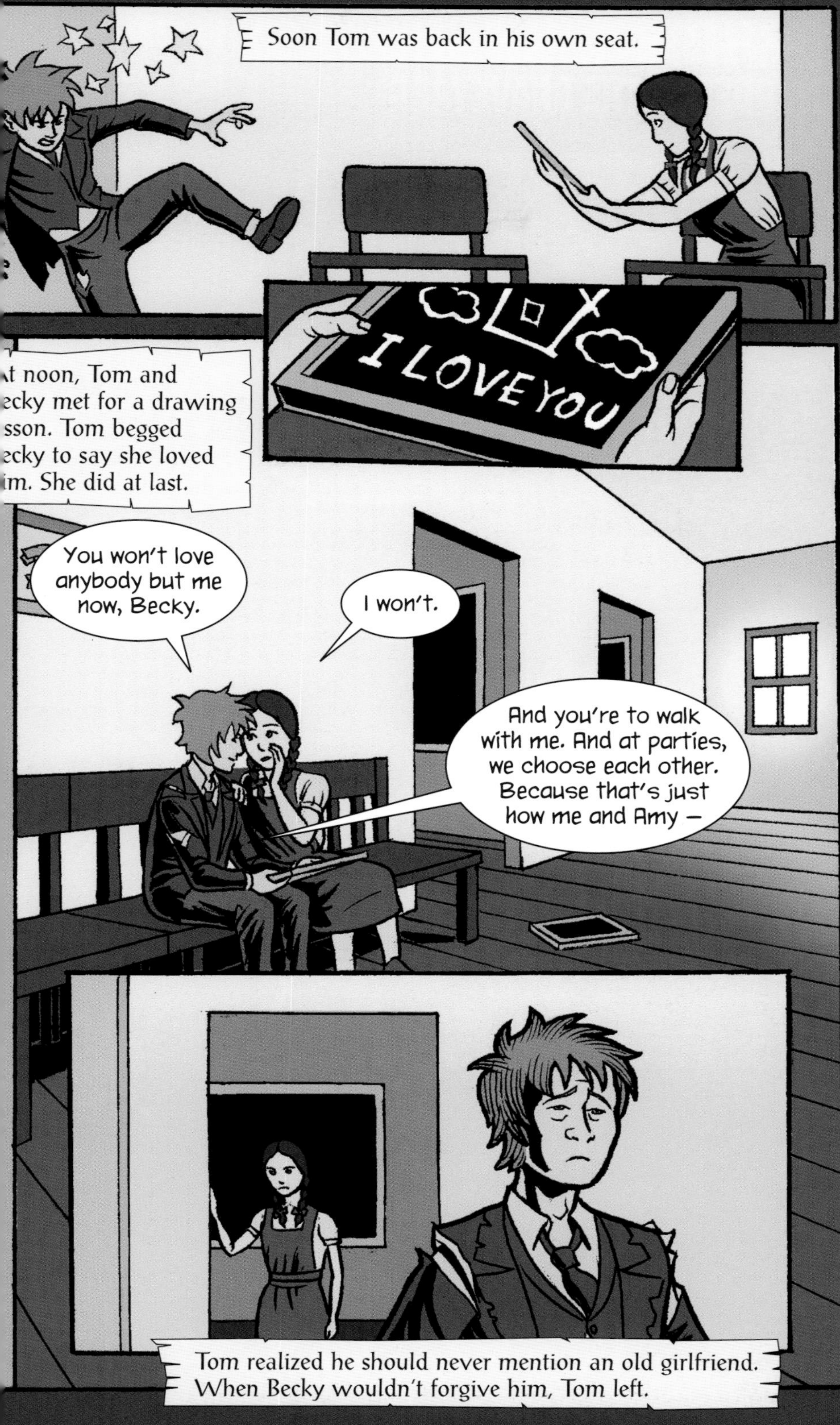
Soon Tom was back in his own seat.
I LOVE YOU
t noon, Tom and ecky met for a drawing sson. Tom begged ecky to say she loved im. She did at last.
You won't love anybody but me now, Becky.
I won't.
And you're to walk with me. And at parties, we choose each other. Because that's just how me and Amy —
Tom realized he should never mention an old girlfriend. When Becky wouldn't forgive him, Tom left.

CHAPTER 2

MURDER IN THE GRAVEYARD

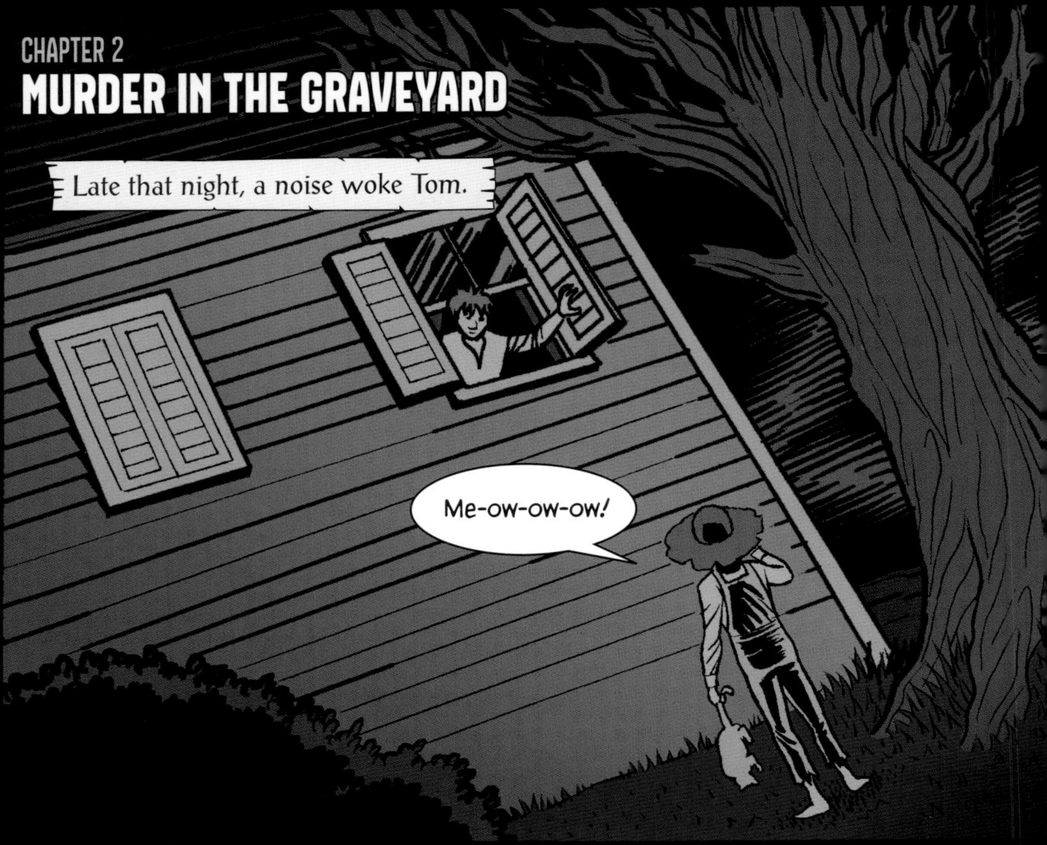
Late that night, a noise woke Tom.
Me-ow-ow-ow!

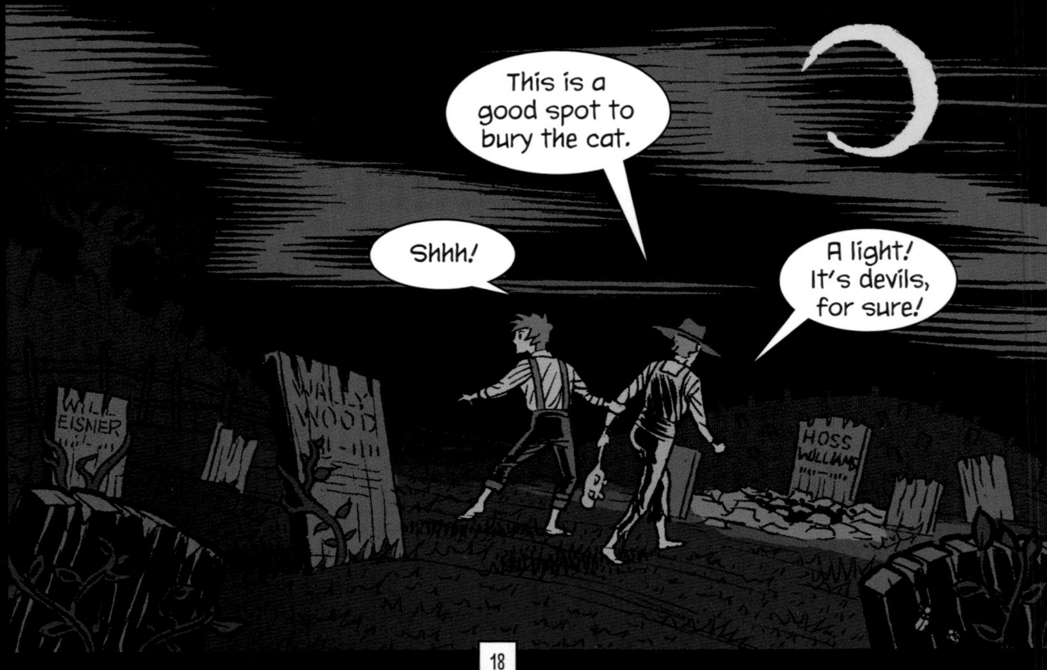
This is a good spot to bury the cat.
Shhh!
A light! It's devils, for sure!

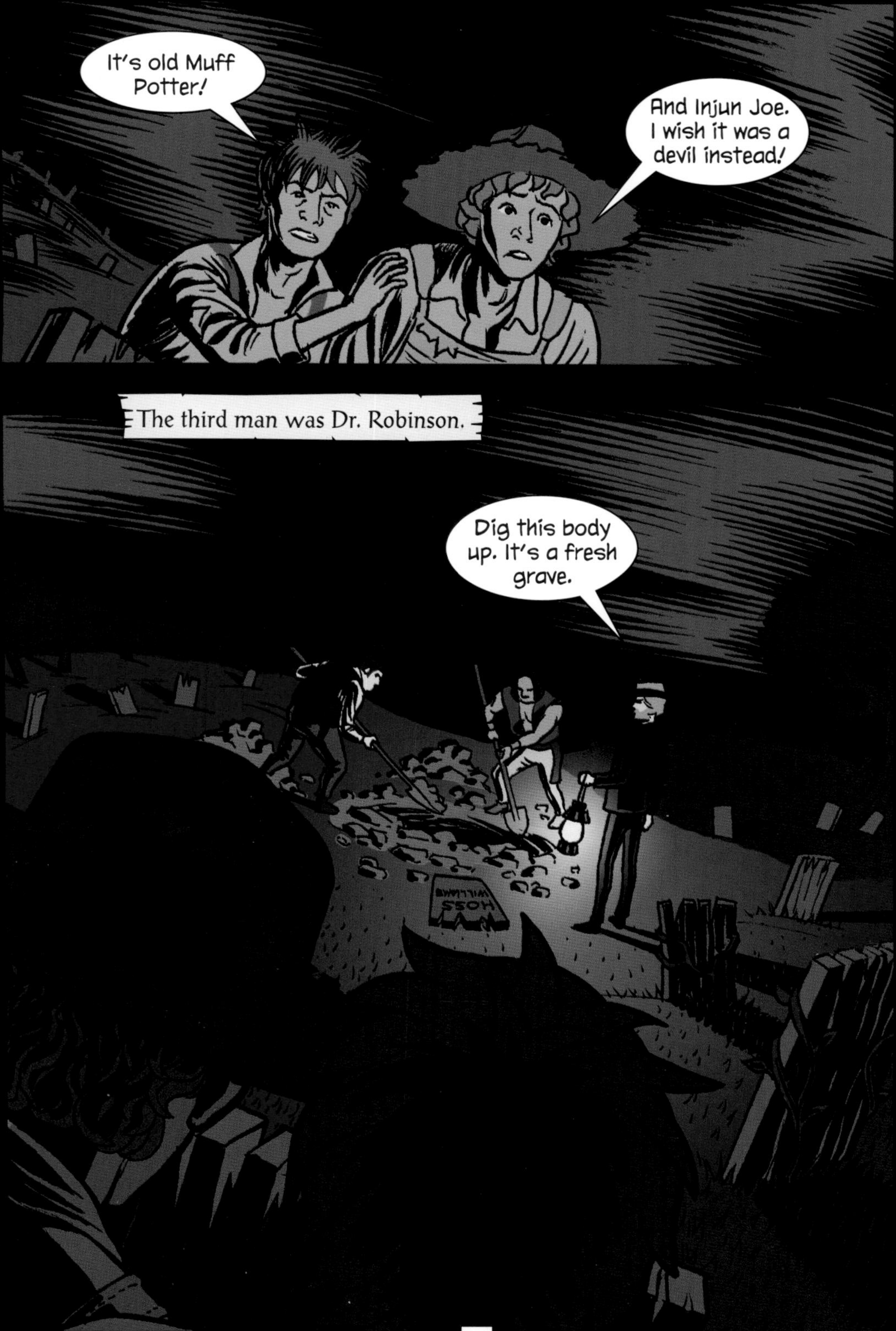
It's old Muff Potter!
And Injun Joe. I wish it was a devil instead!
The third man was Dr. Robinson.
Dig this body up. It's a fresh grave.

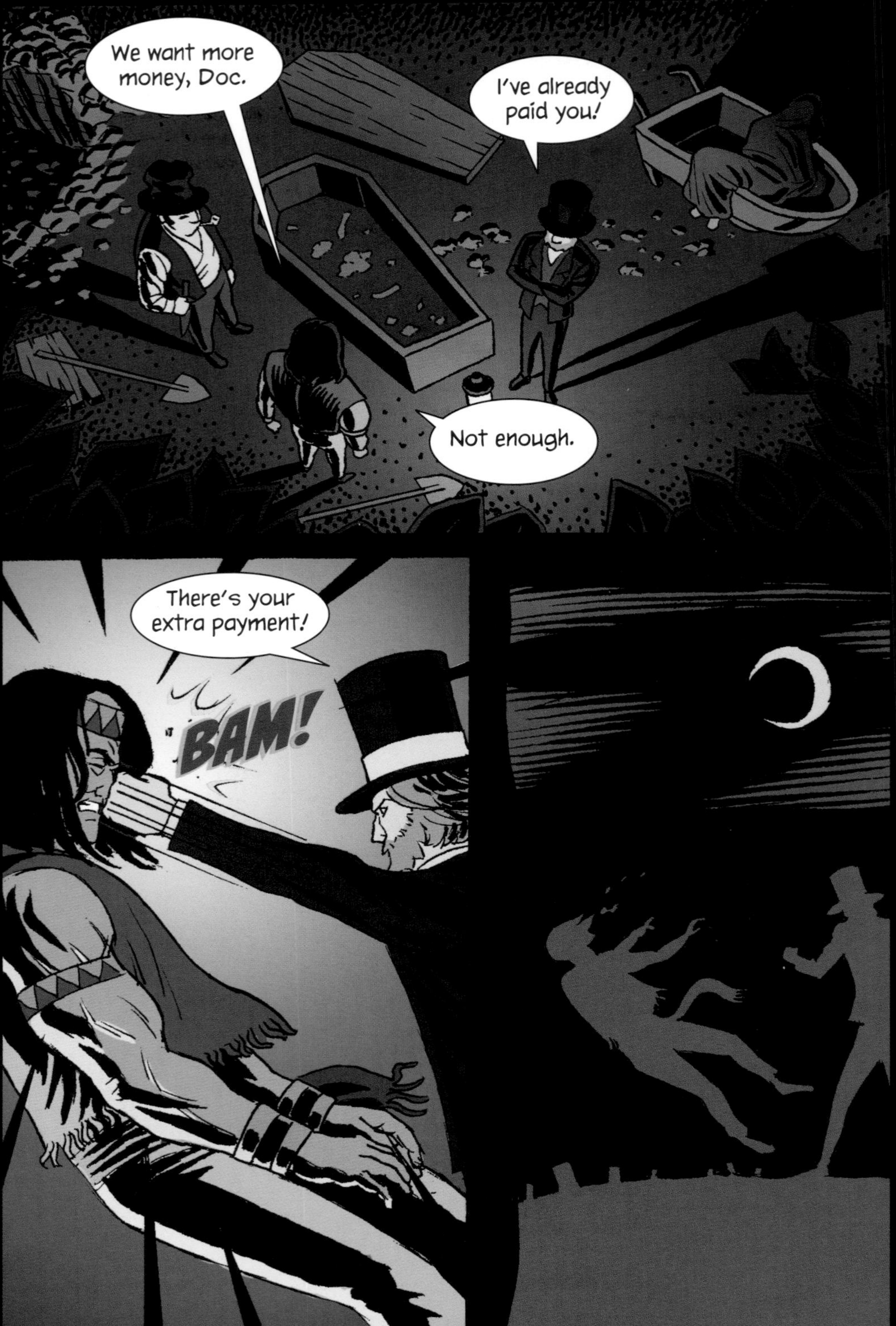

We want more money, Doc.
I've already paid you!
Not enough.
There's your extra payment!
BAM!

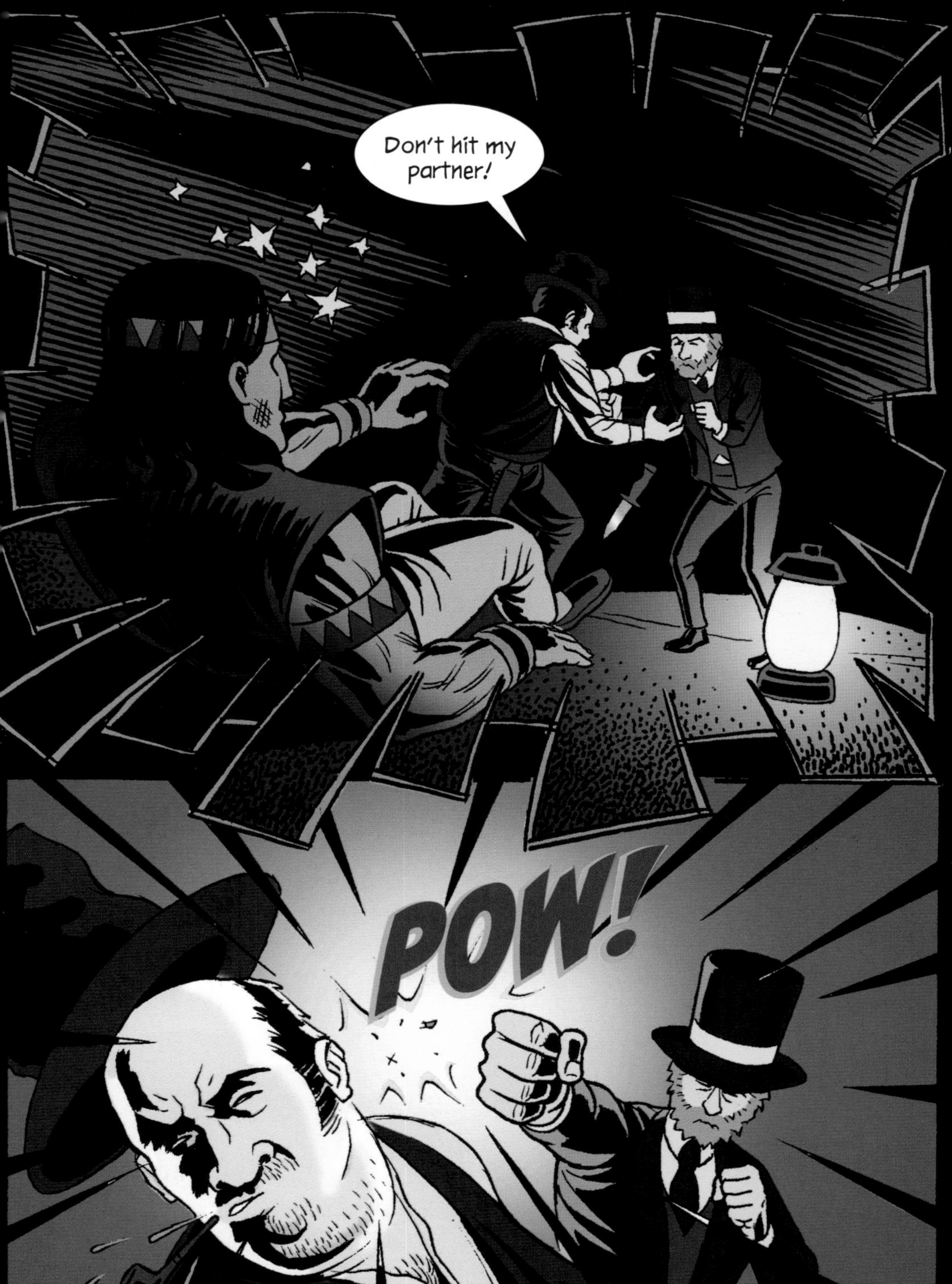
Don't hit my partner!
POW!

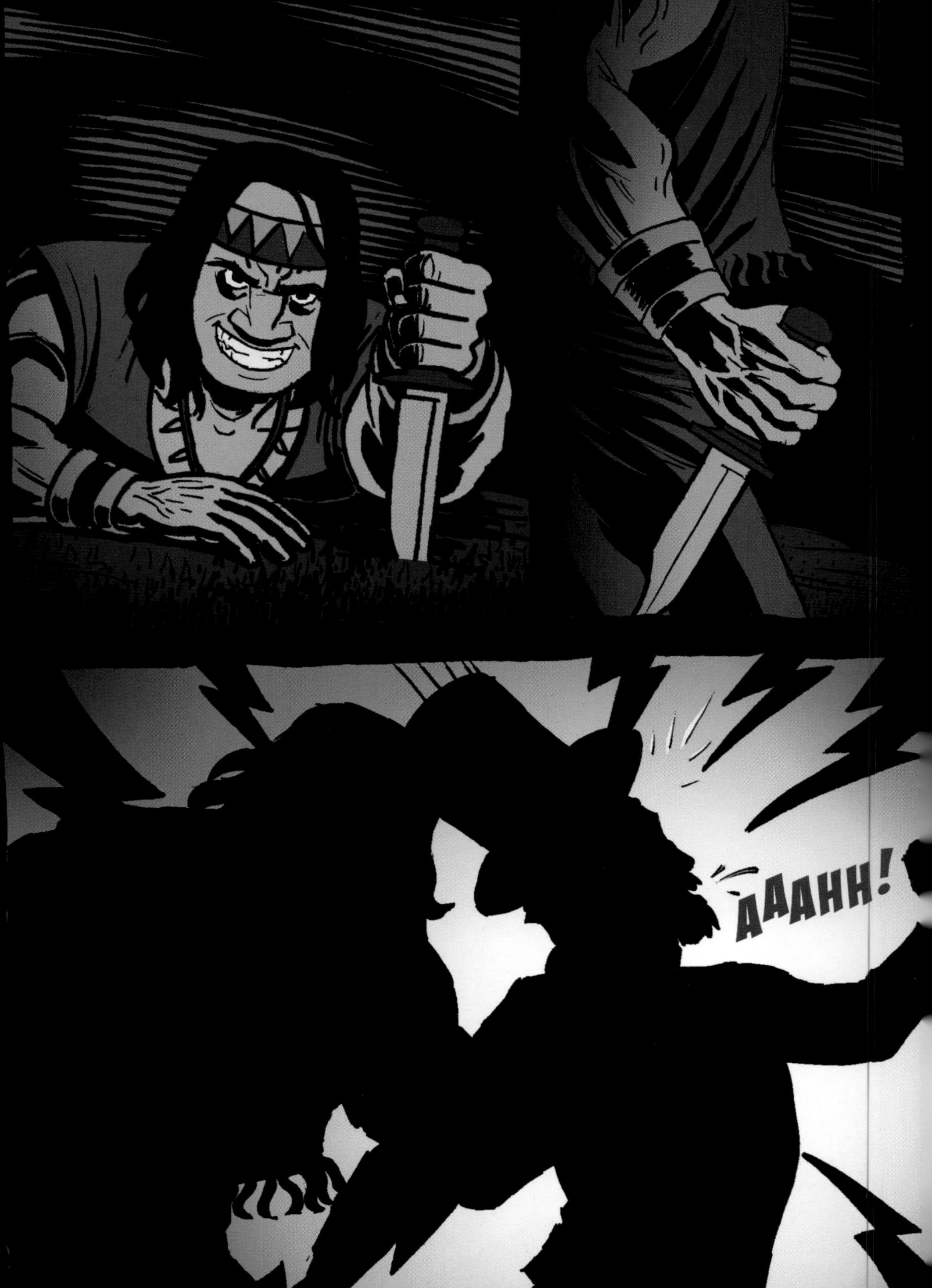
AAAHH!

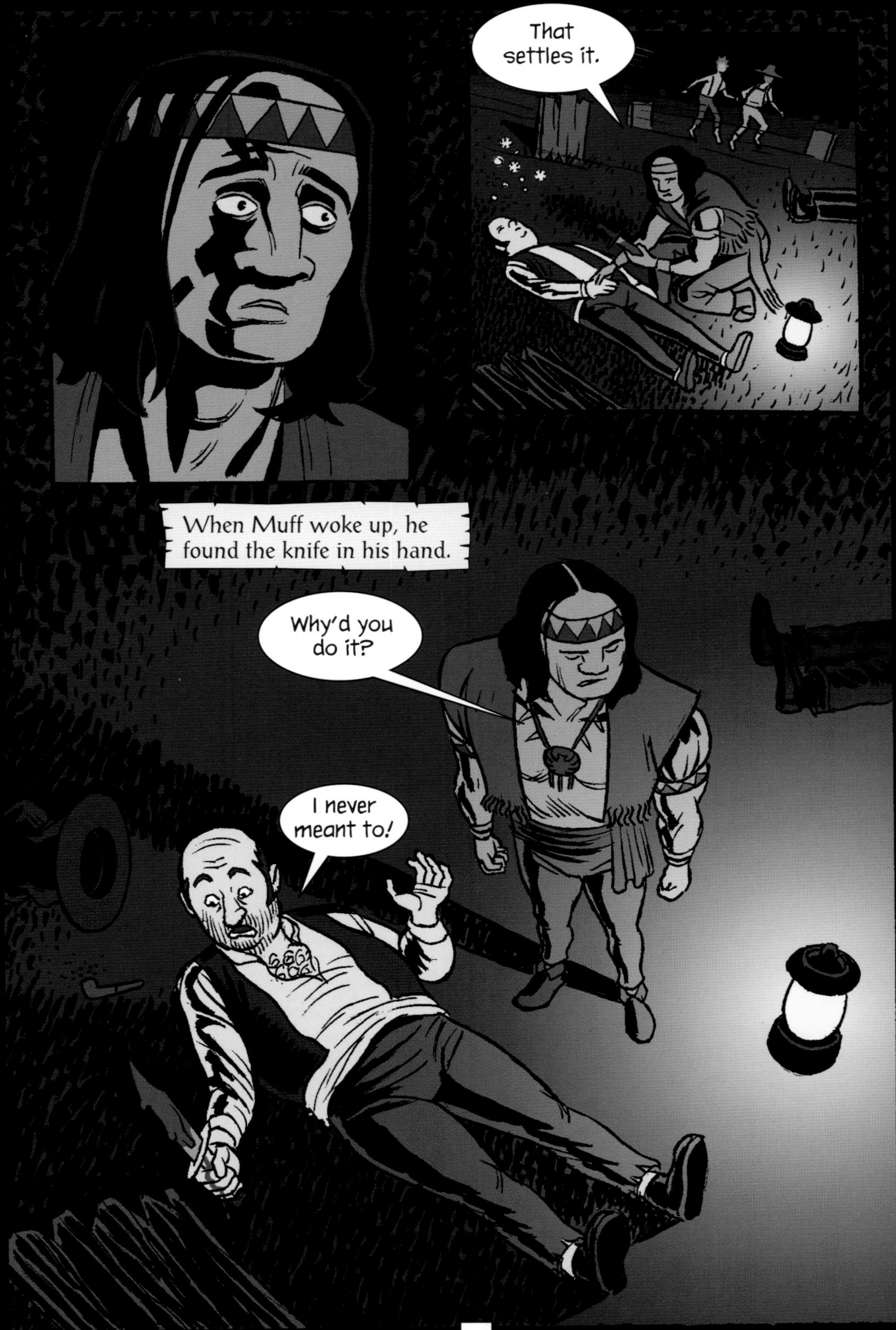
That settles it.
When Muff woke up, he found the knife in his hand.
Why'd you do it?
I never meant to!

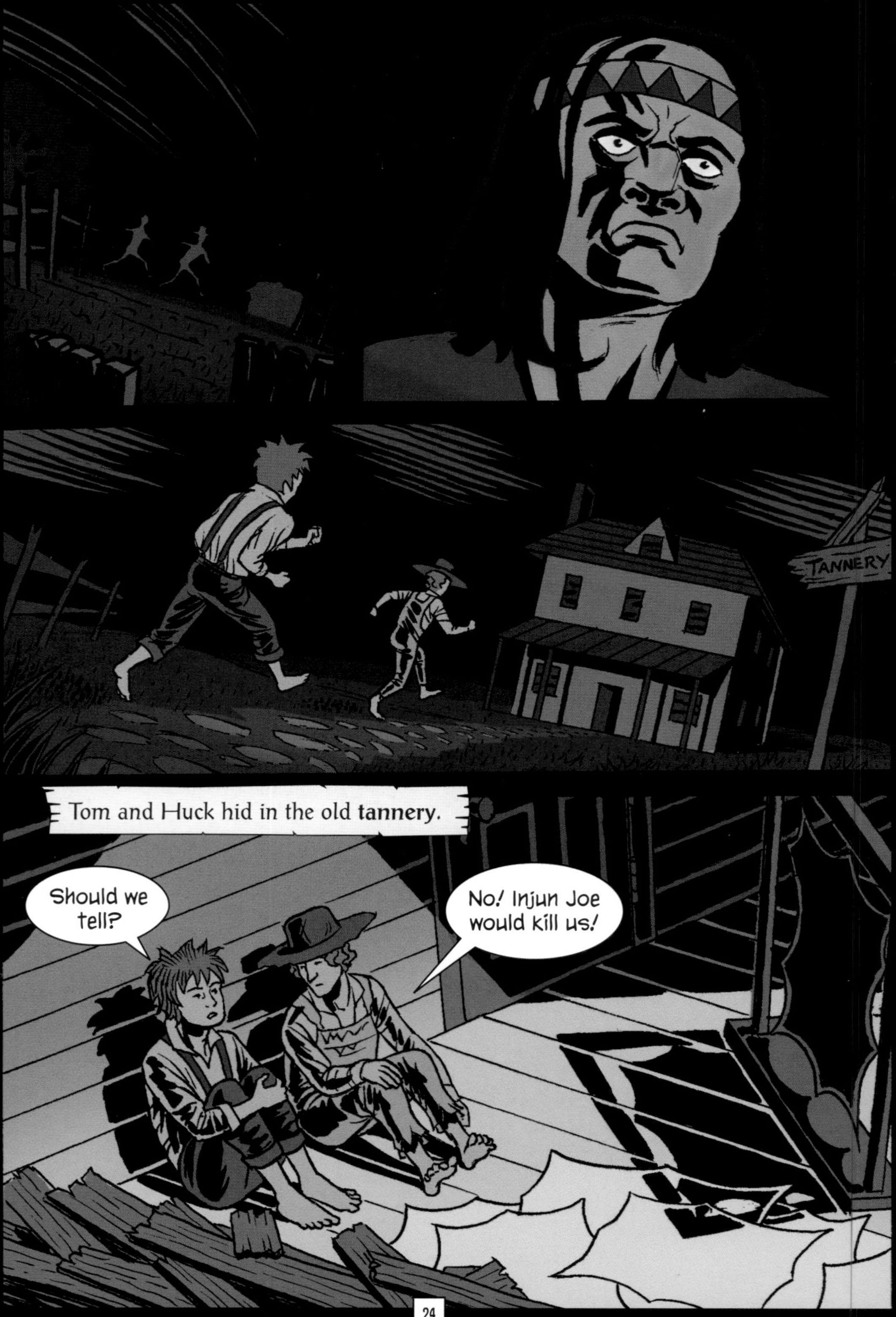
TANNERY
Tom and Huck hid in the old tannery.
Should we tell?
No! Injun Joe would kill us!

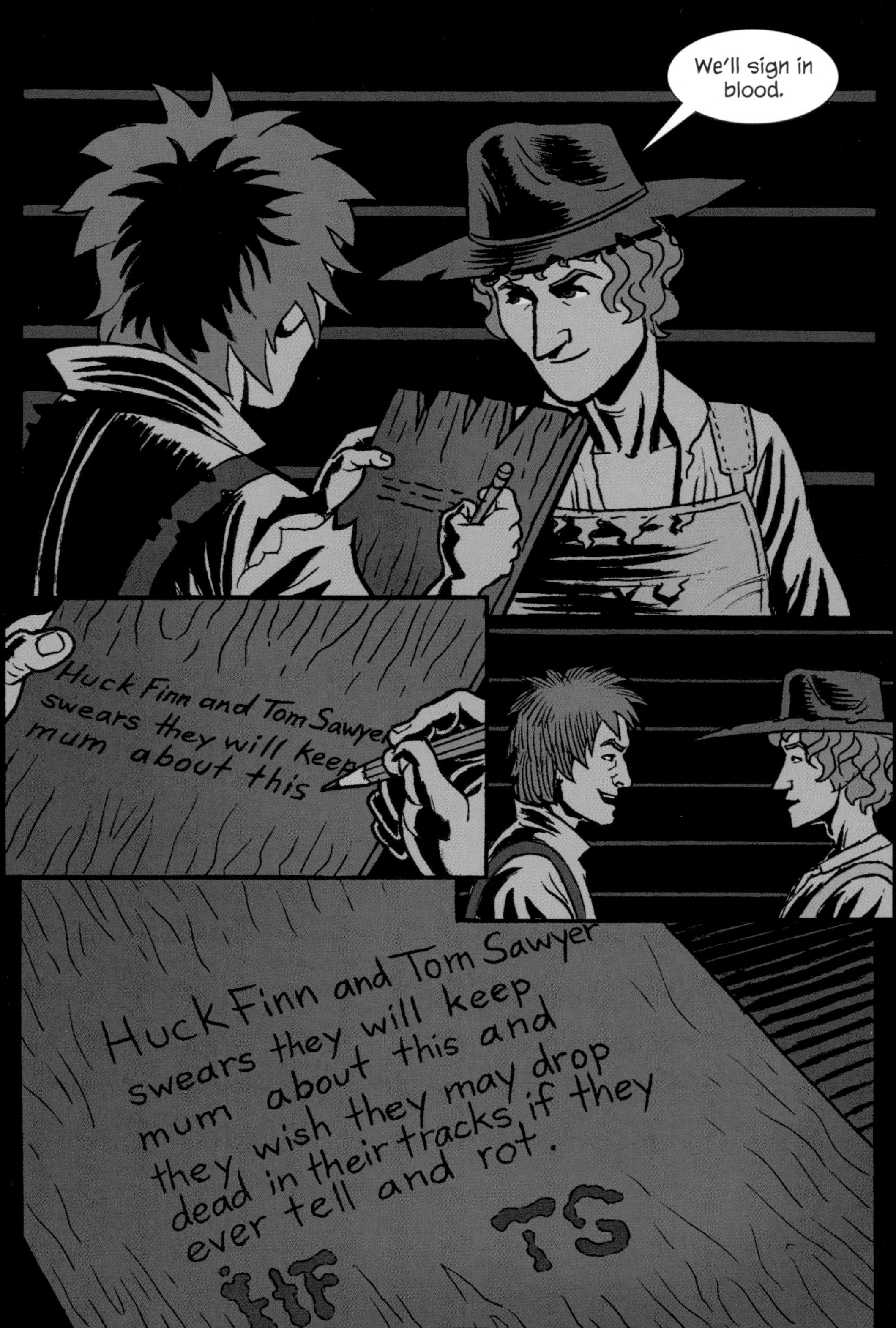
We'll sign in blood.
Huck Finn and Tom Sawyer swears they will keep mum about this
Huck Finn and Tom Sawyer swears they will keep mum about this and they wish they may drop dead in their tracks if they ever tell and rot.
HF
TS

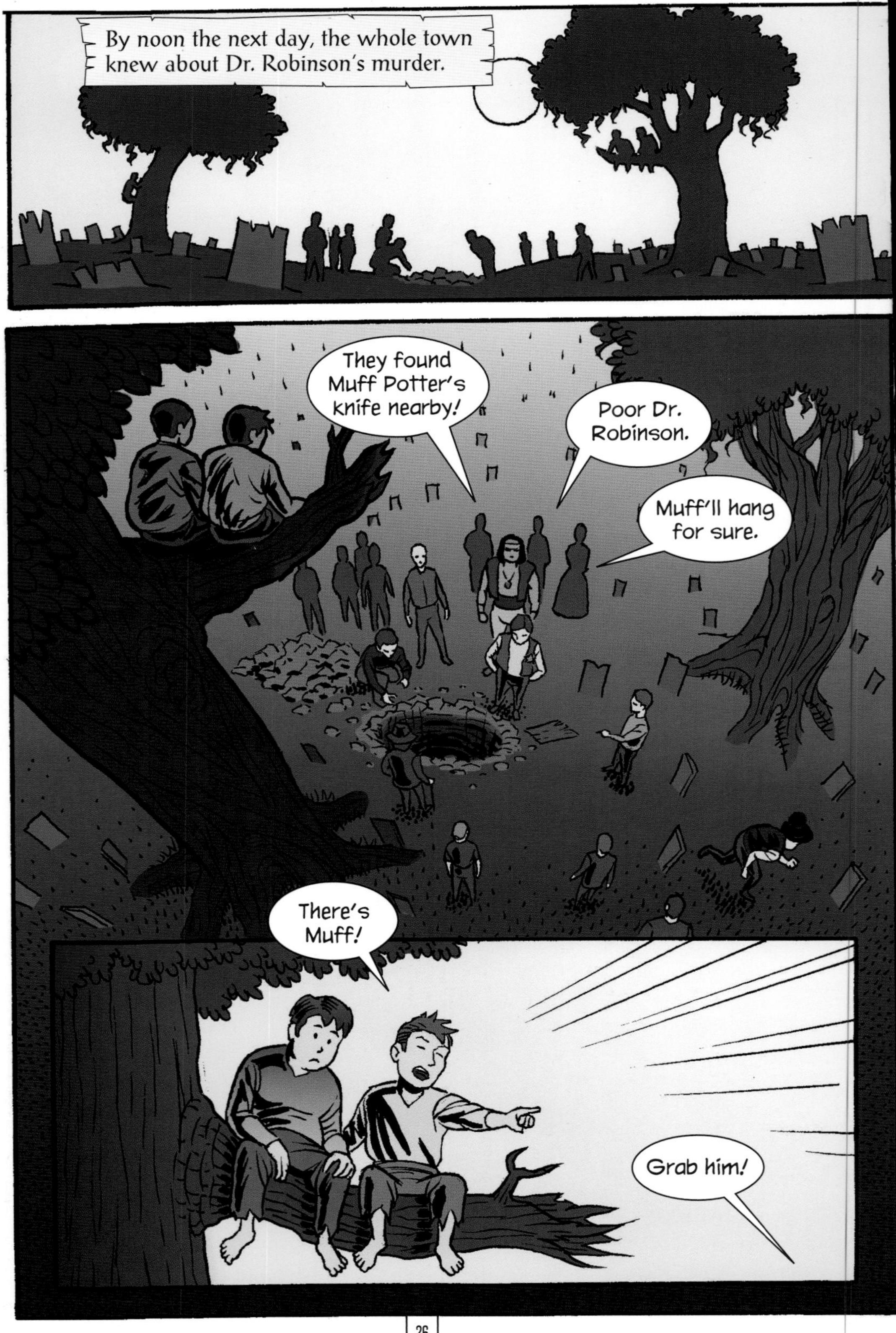
By noon the next day, the whole town knew about Dr. Robinson's murder.
They found Muff Potter's knife nearby!
Poor Dr. Robinson.
Muff'll hang for sure.
There's Muff!
Grab him!

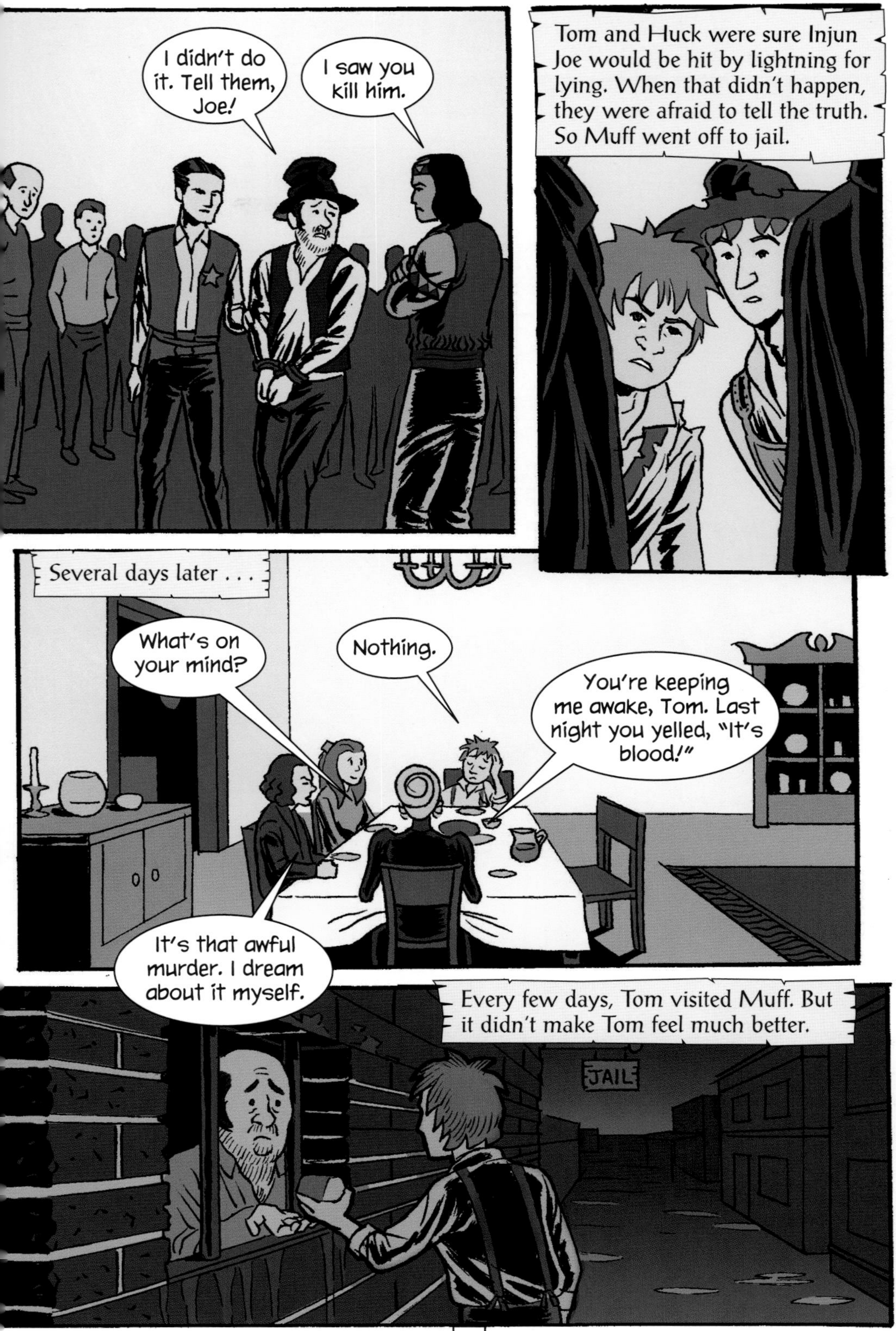
I didn't do it. Tell them, Joe!
I saw you kill him.
Tom and Huck were sure Injun Joe would be hit by lightning for lying. When that didn't happen, they were afraid to tell the truth. So Muff went off to jail.
Several days later . . .
What's on your mind?
Nothing.
You're keeping me awake, Tom. Last night you yelled, "It's blood!"
It's that awful murder. I dream about it myself.
Every few days, Tom visited Muff. But it didn't make Tom feel much better.
JAIL

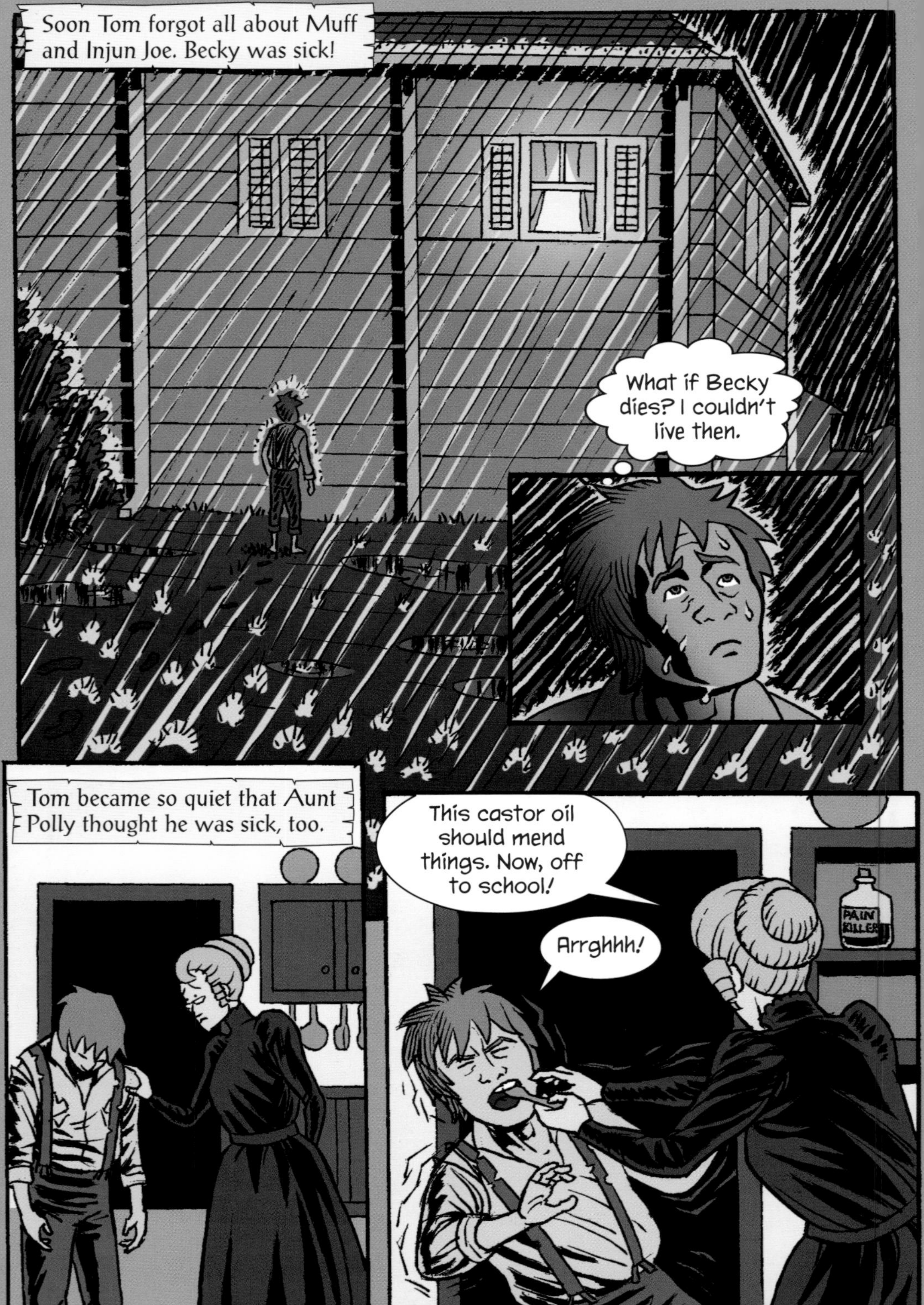
Soon Tom forgot all about Muff and Injun Joe. Becky was sick!
What if Becky dies? I couldn't live then.
Tom became so quiet that Aunt Polly thought he was sick, too.
This castor oil should mend things. Now, off to school!
Arrghhh!
PAIN KILLER

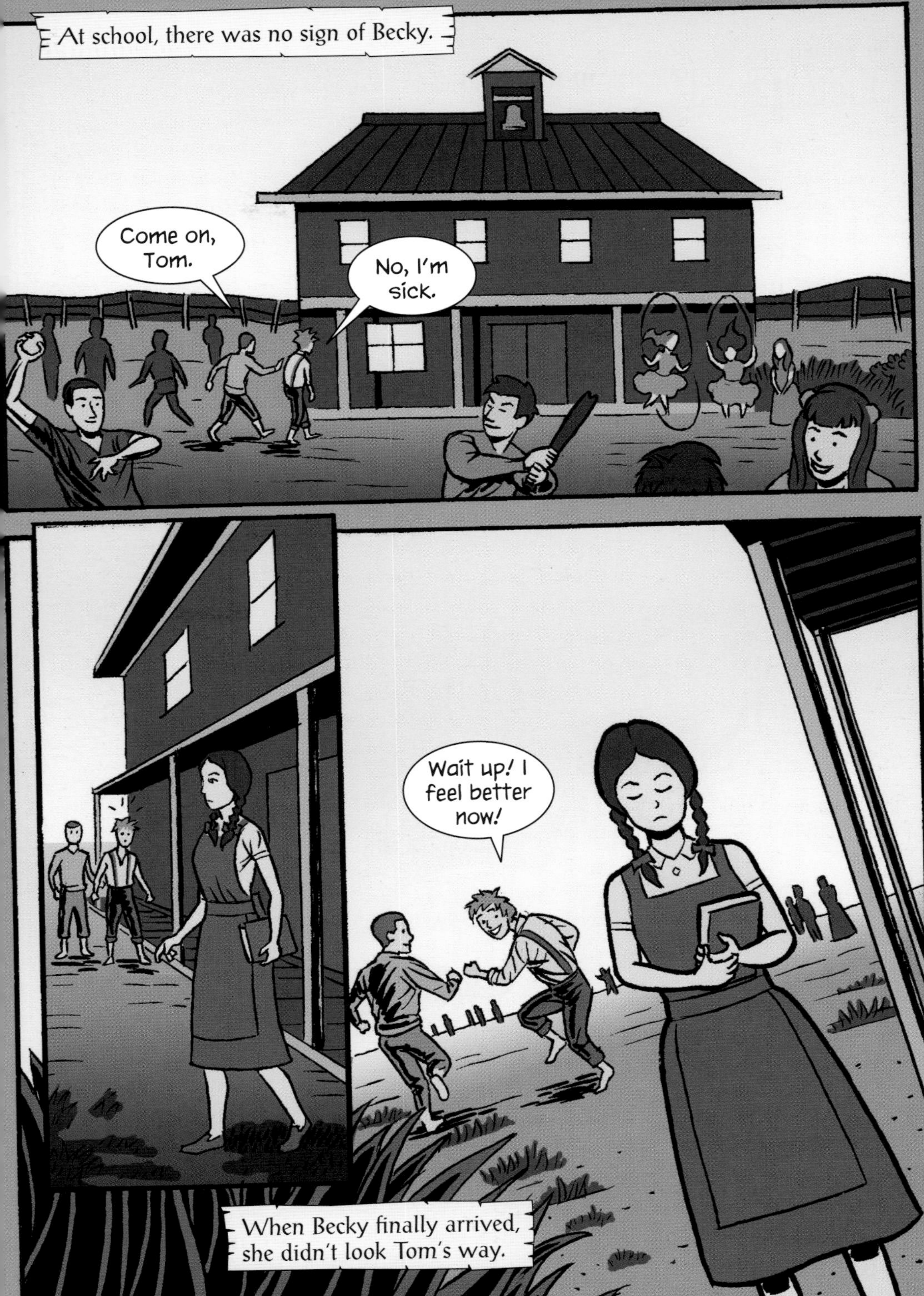
At school, there was no sign of Becky.
Come on, Tom.
No, I'm sick.
When Becky finally arrived, she didn't look Tom's way.
Wait up! I feel better now!

CHAPTER 3
A PIRATE'S LIFE

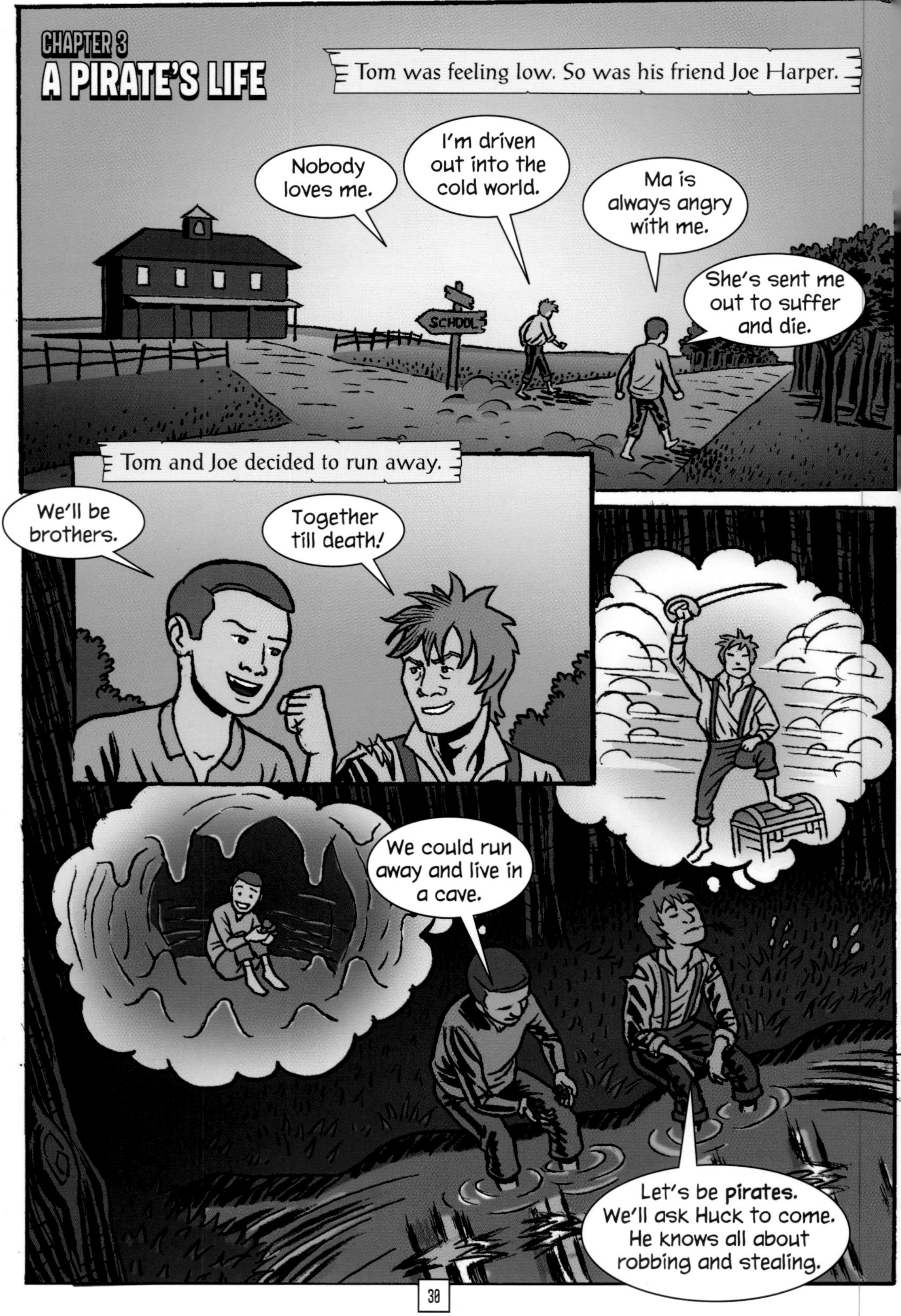
Tom was feeling low. So was his friend Joe Harper.
Nobody loves me.
I'm driven out into the cold world.
Ma is always angry with me.
She's sent me out to suffer and die.
SCHOOL
Tom and Joe decided to run away.
We'll be brothers.
Together till death!
We could run away and live in a cave.
Let's be **pirates**. We'll ask Huck to come. He knows all about robbing and stealing.

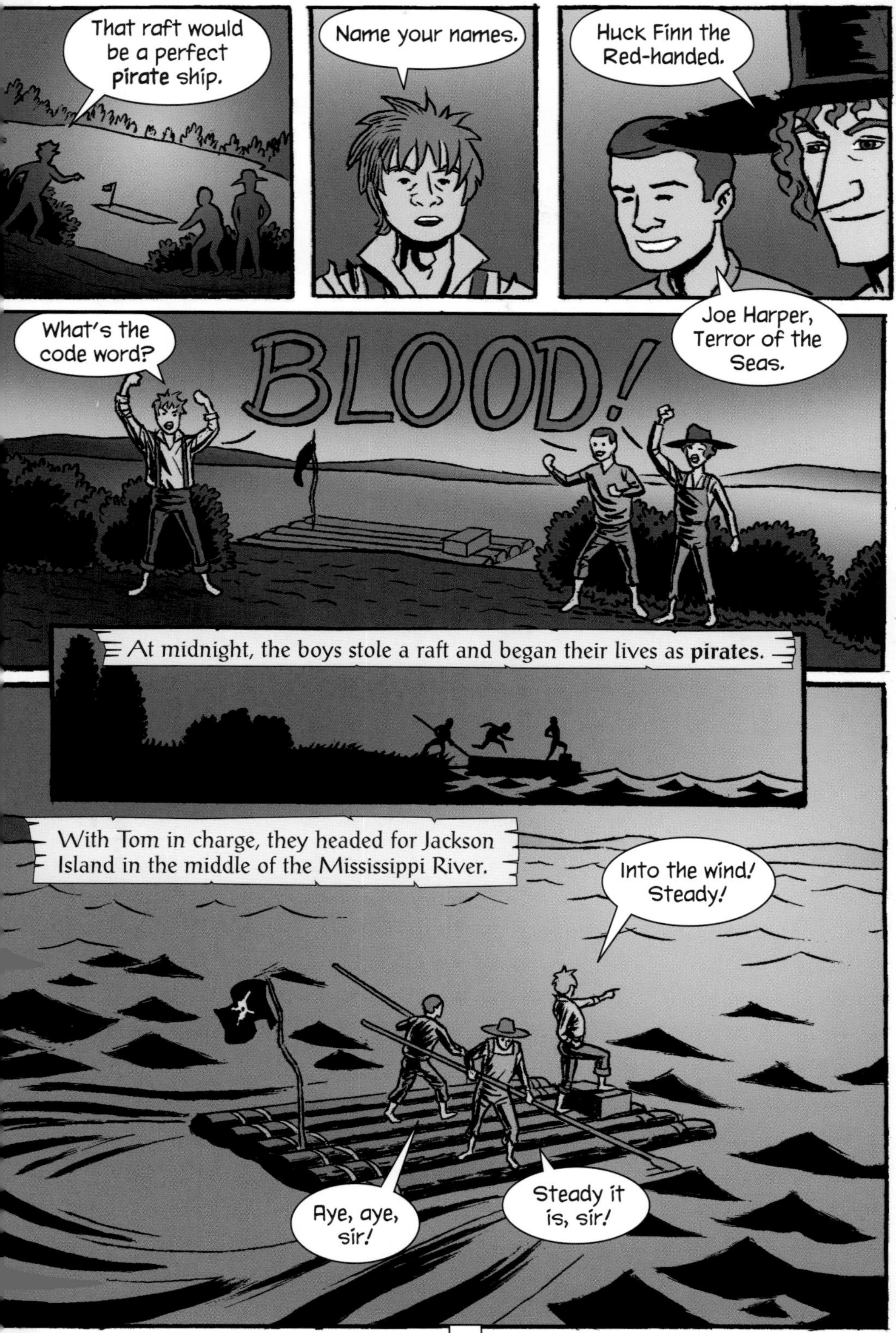
That raft would be a perfect **pirate** ship.
Name your names.
Huck Finn the Red-handed.
Joe Harper, Terror of the Seas.
What's the code word?
BLOOD!
At midnight, the boys stole a raft and began their lives as **pirates**.
With Tom in charge, they headed for Jackson Island in the middle of the Mississippi River.
Into the wind! Steady!
Aye, aye, sir!
Steady it is, sir!

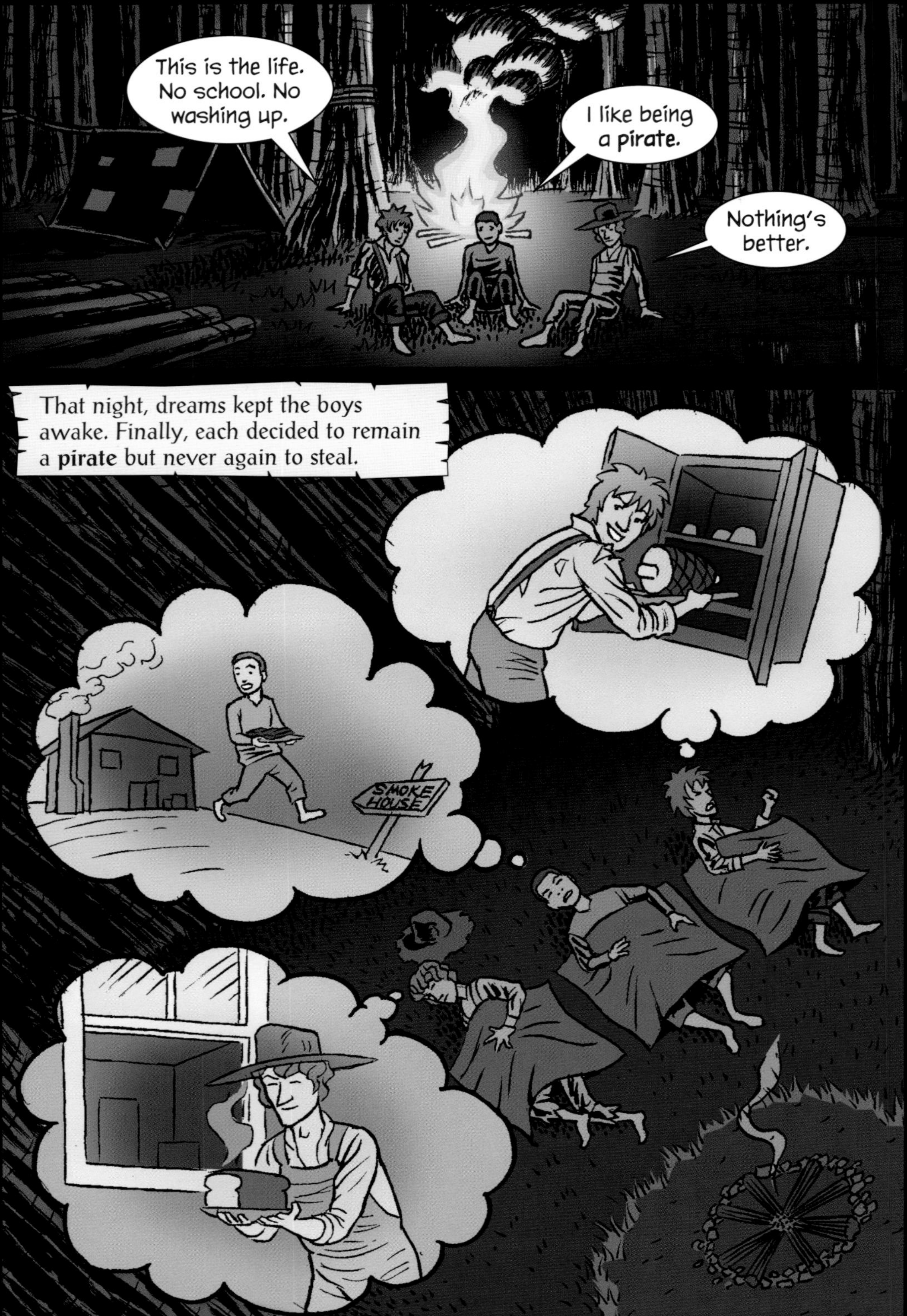
This is the life. No school. No washing up.
I like being a pirate.
Nothing's better.
That night, dreams kept the boys awake. Finally, each decided to remain a pirate but never again to steal.
SMOKE HOUSE

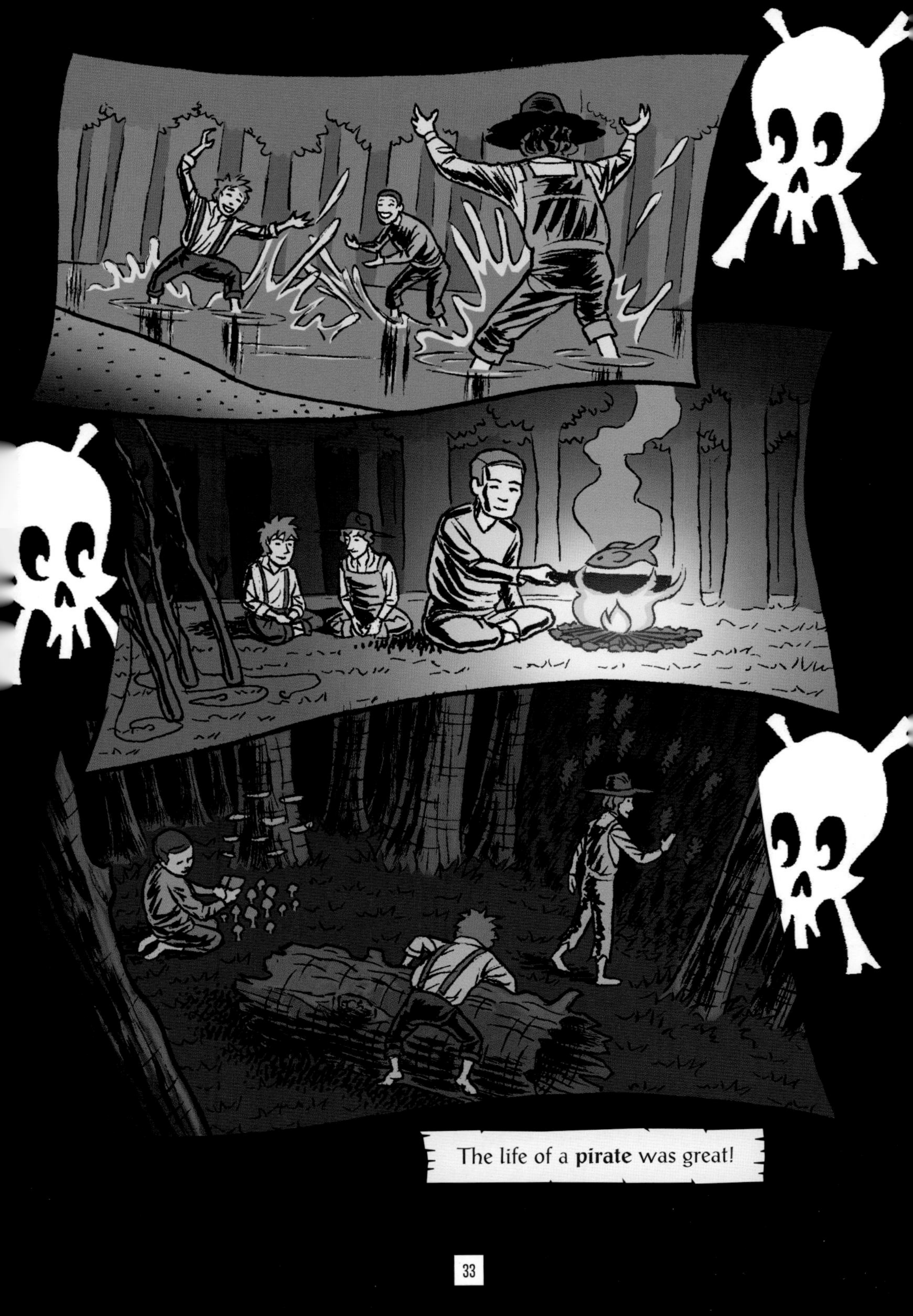
The life of a **pirate** was great!

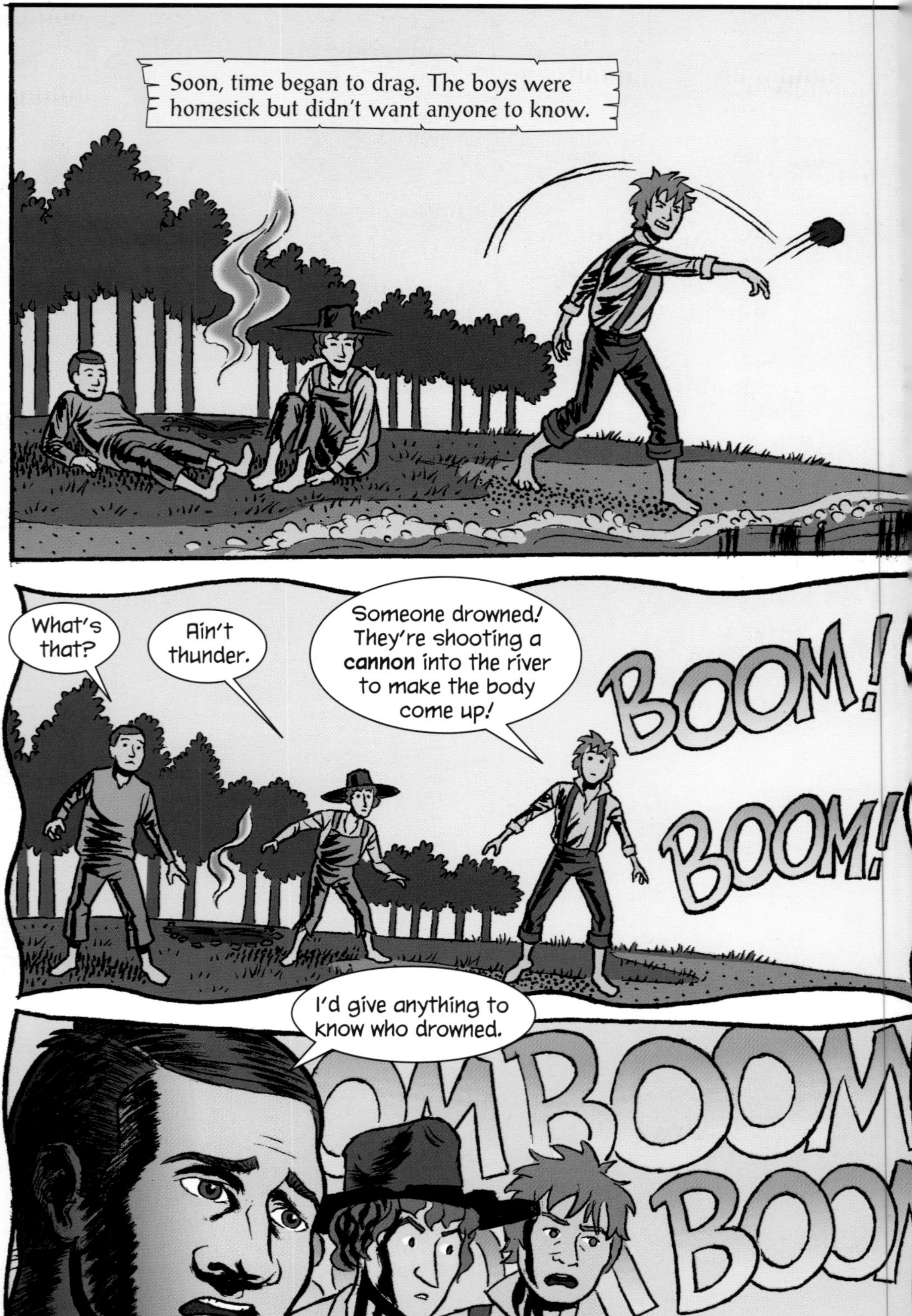
Soon, time began to drag. The boys were homesick but didn't want anyone to know.
What's that?
Ain't thunder.
Someone drowned! They're shooting a **cannon** into the river to make the body come up!
BOOM!
BOOM!
I'd give anything to know who drowned.
BOOM
BOOM

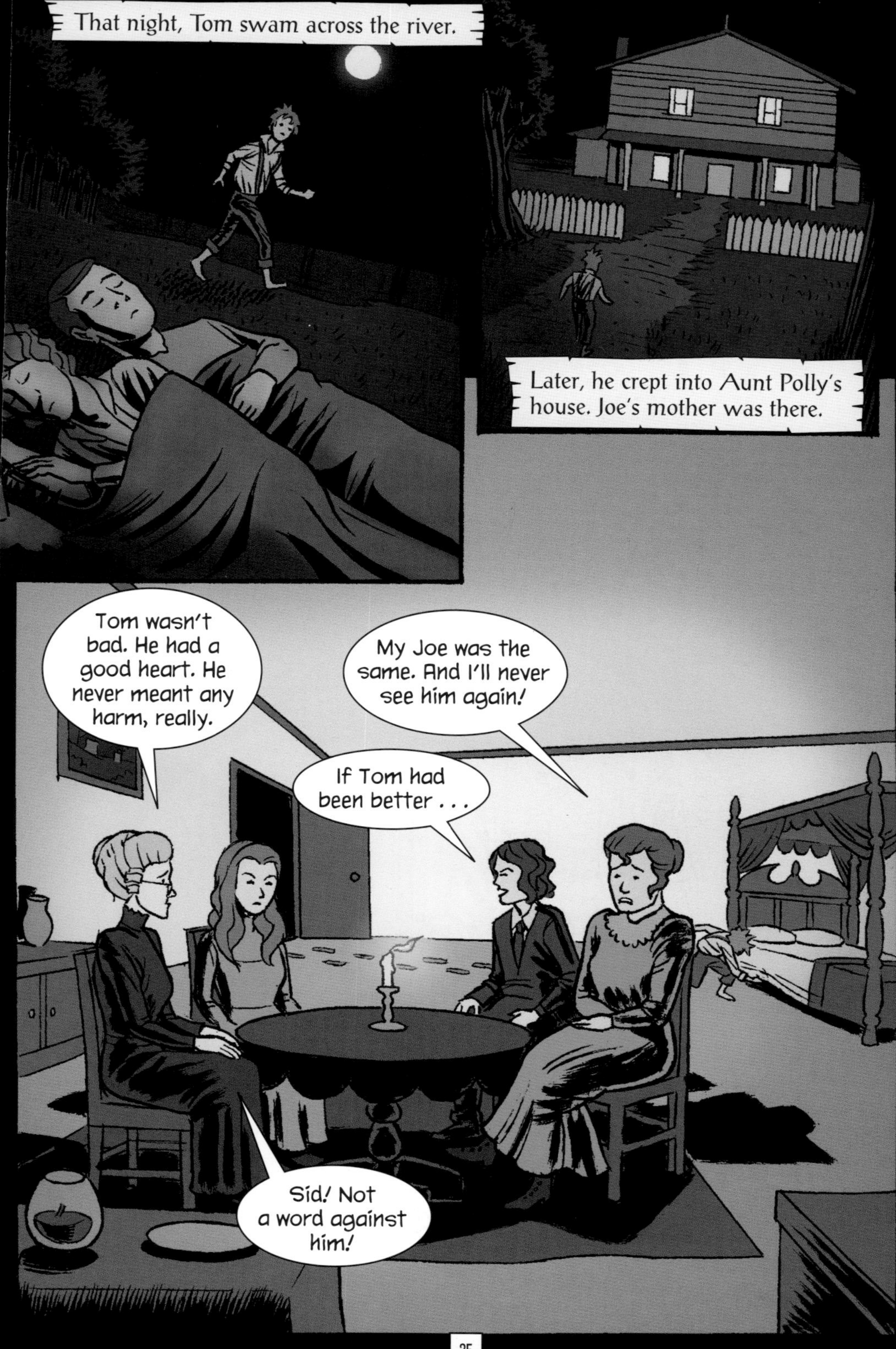

That night, Tom swam across the river.
Later, he crept into Aunt Polly's house. Joe's mother was there.
Tom wasn't bad. He had a good heart. He never meant any harm, really.
My Joe was the same. And I'll never see him again!
If Tom had been better . . .
Sid! Not a word against him!

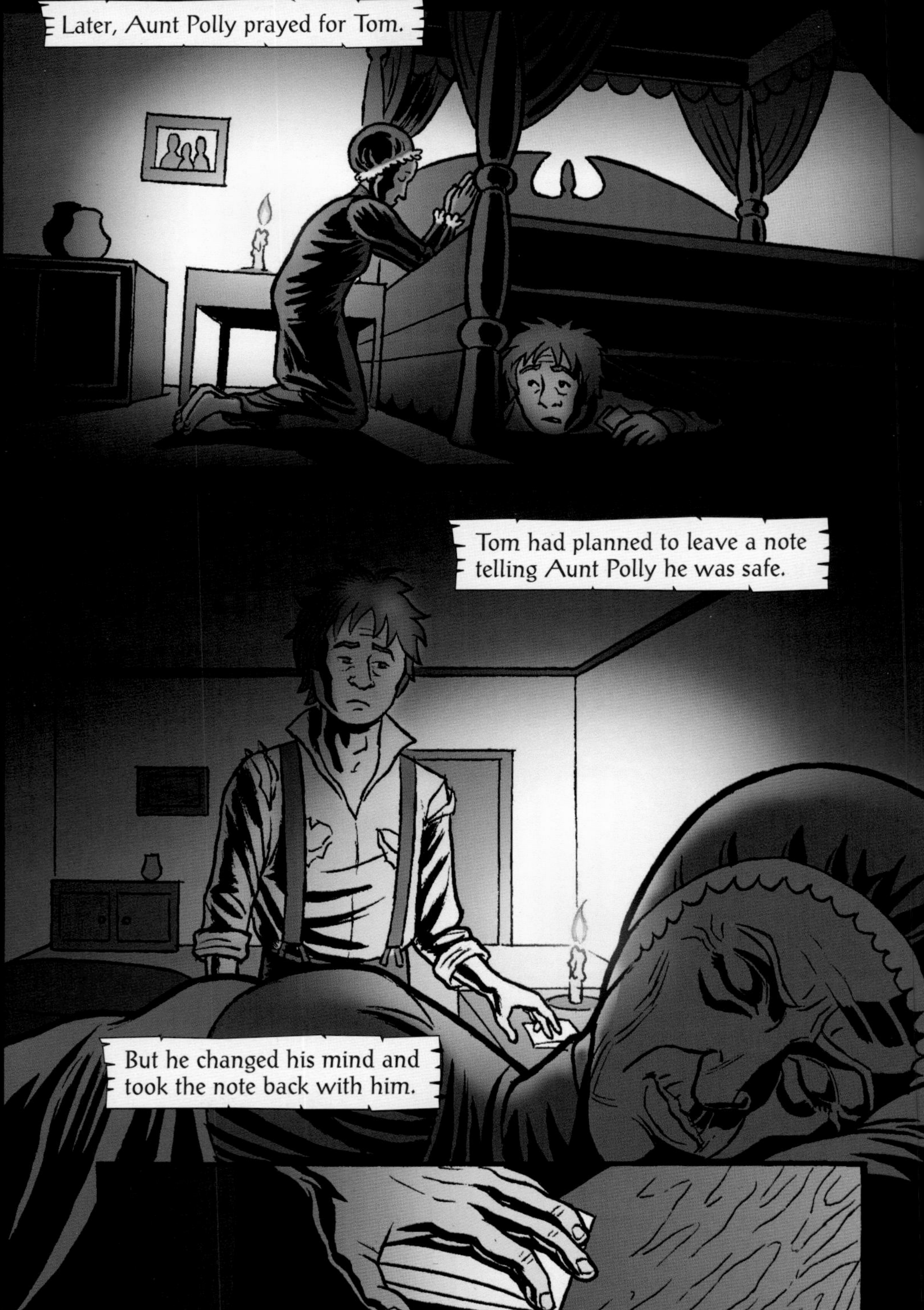

Later, Aunt Polly prayed for Tom.
Tom had planned to leave a note telling Aunt Polly he was safe.
But he changed his mind and took the note back with him.

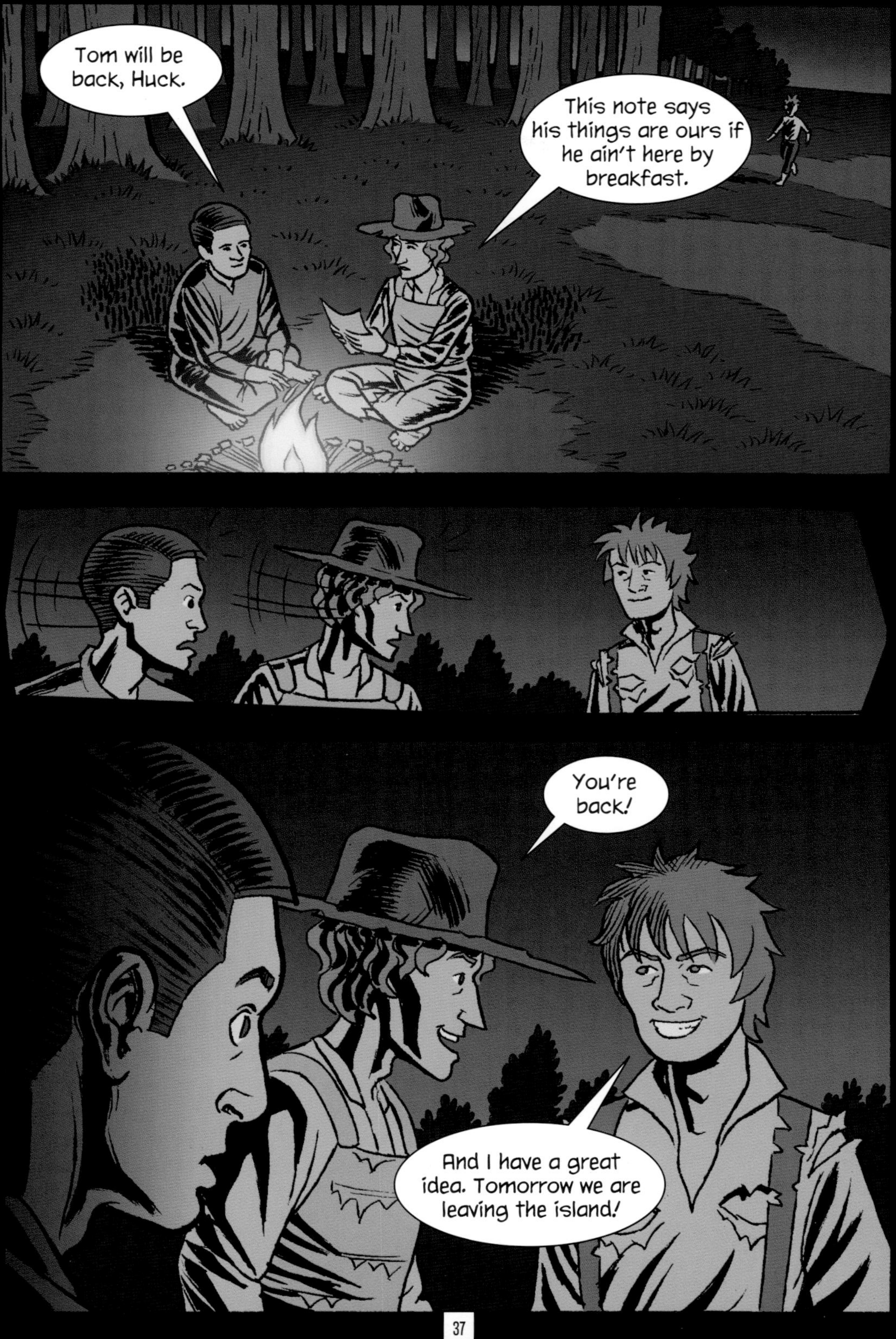
Tom will be back, Huck.
This note says his things are ours if he ain't here by breakfast.
You're back!
And I have a great idea. Tomorrow we are leaving the island!

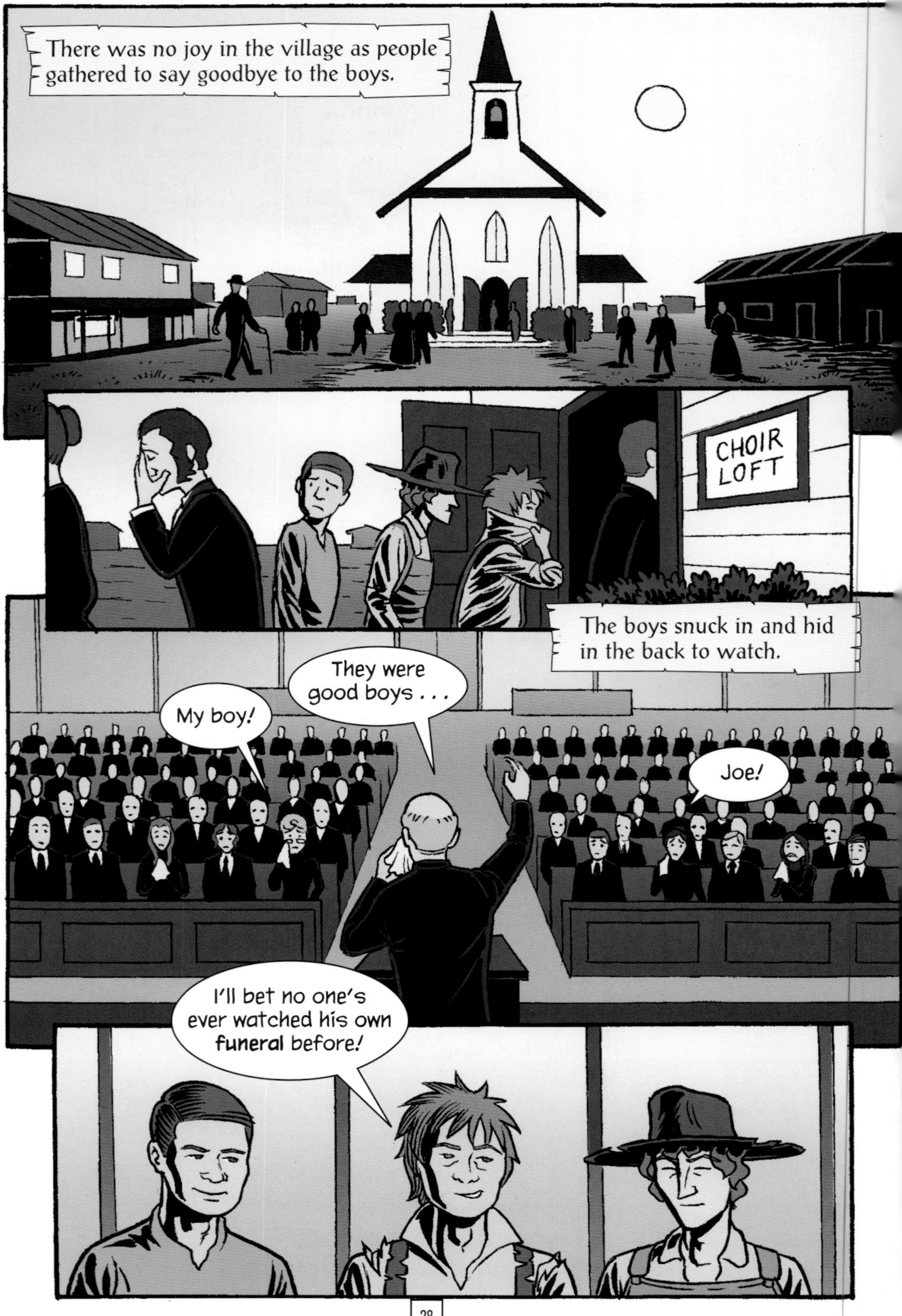
There was no joy in the village as people gathered to say goodbye to the boys.
CHOIR LOFT
The boys snuck in and hid in the back to watch.
My boy!
They were good boys . . .
Joe!
I'll bet no one's ever watched his own **funeral** before!

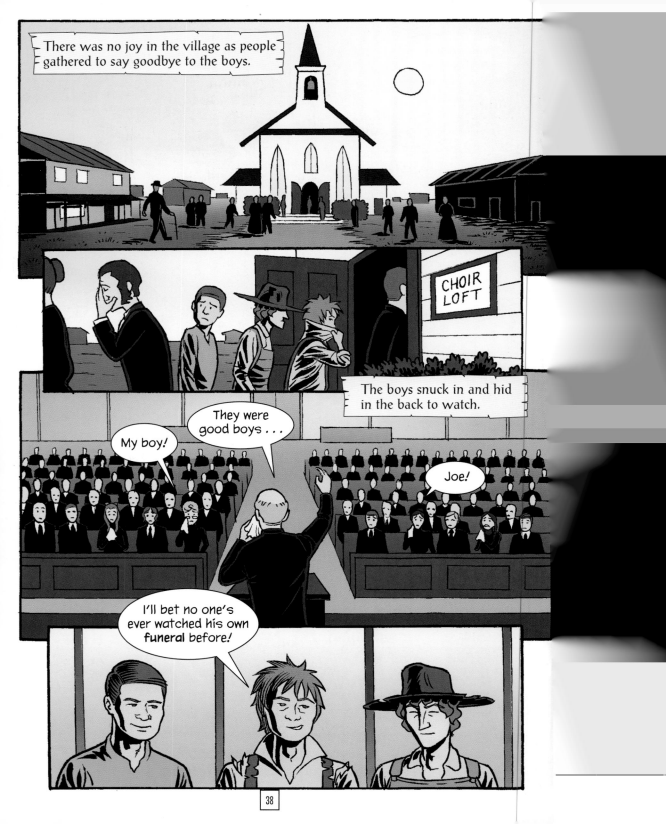

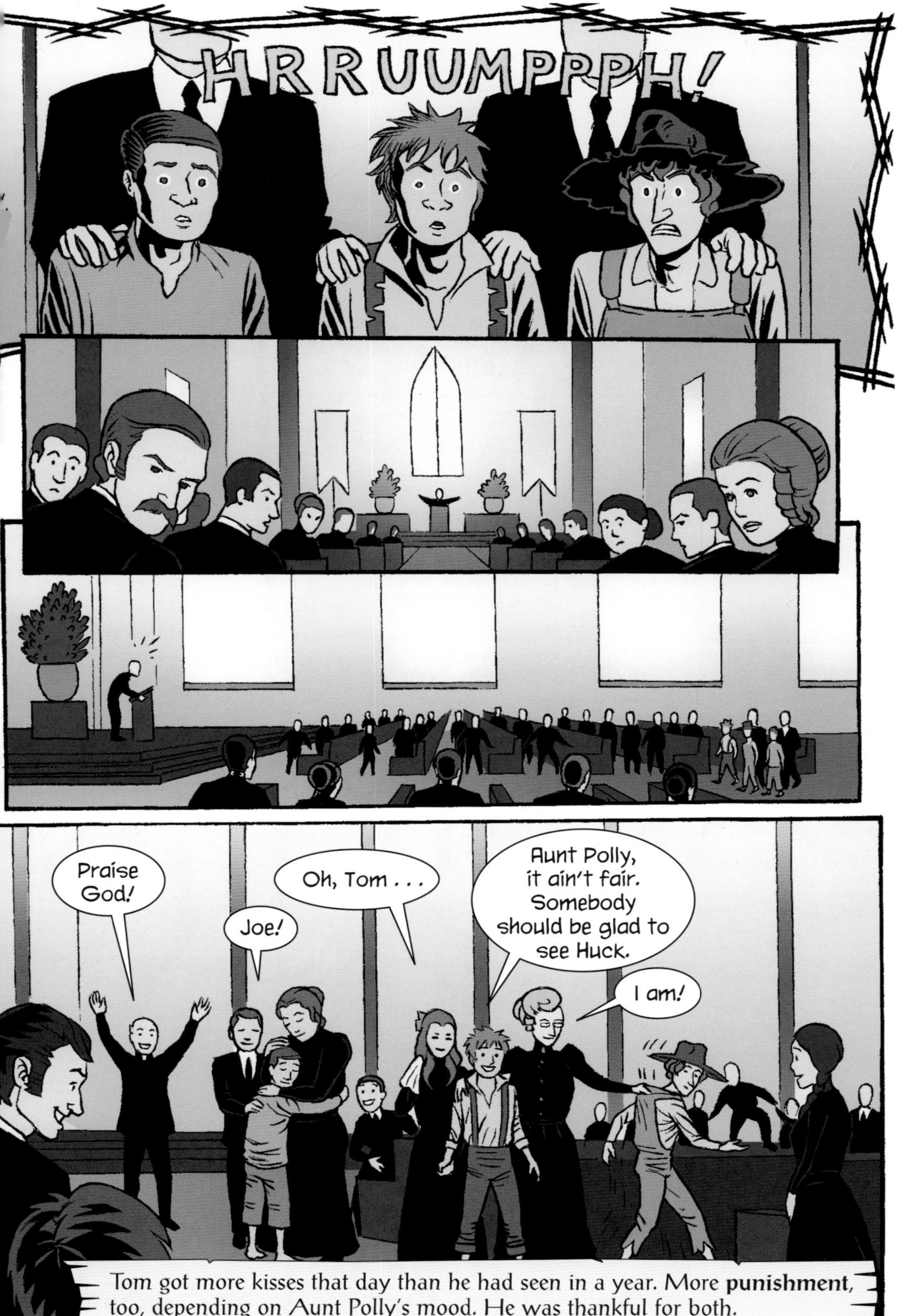
HRRUUMPPPH!
Praise God!
Joe!
Oh, Tom . . .
Aunt Polly, it ain't fair. Somebody should be glad to see Huck.
I am!
Tom got more kisses that day than he had seen in a year. More **punishment**, too, depending on Aunt Polly's mood. He was thankful for both.

CHAPTER 4
MORE TROUBLE FOR TOM

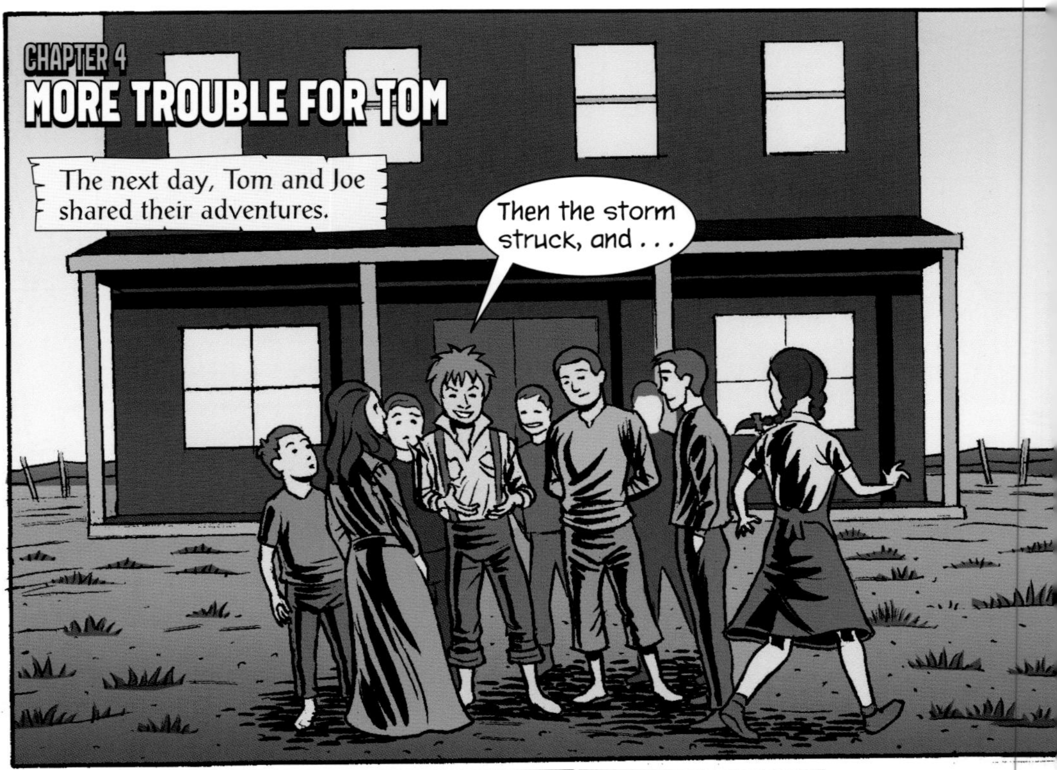
The next day, Tom and Joe shared their adventures.
Then the storm struck, and . . .

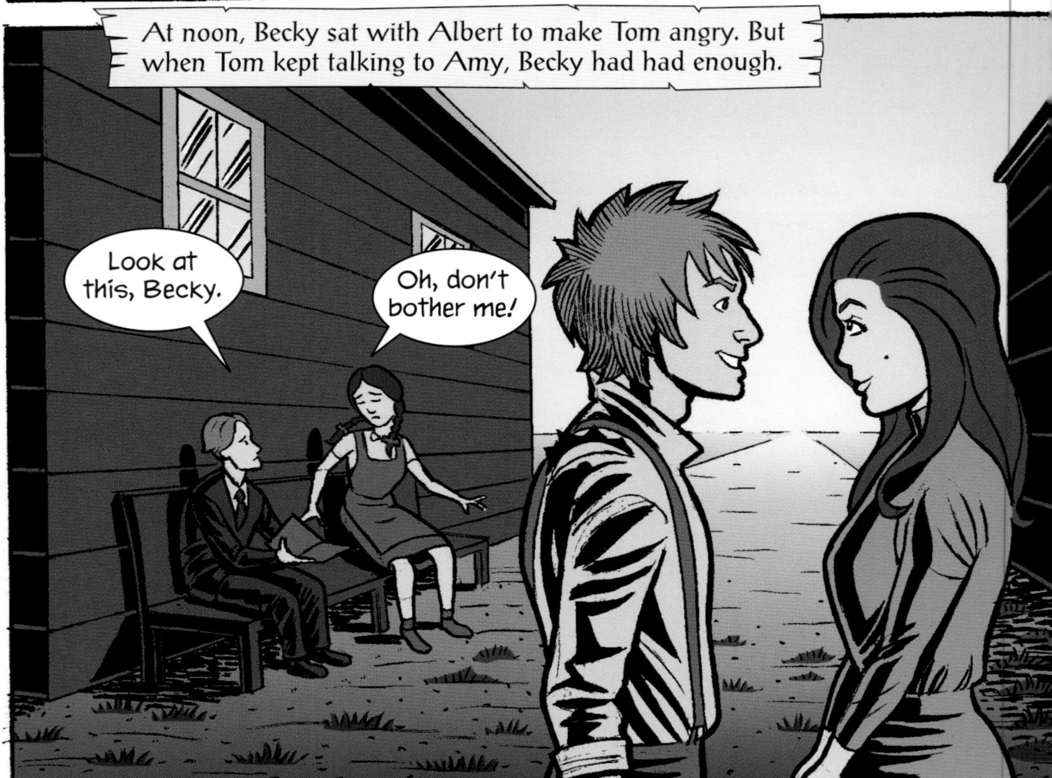
At noon, Becky sat with Albert to make Tom angry. But when Tom kept talking to Amy, Becky had had enough.
Look at this, Becky.
Oh, don't bother me!

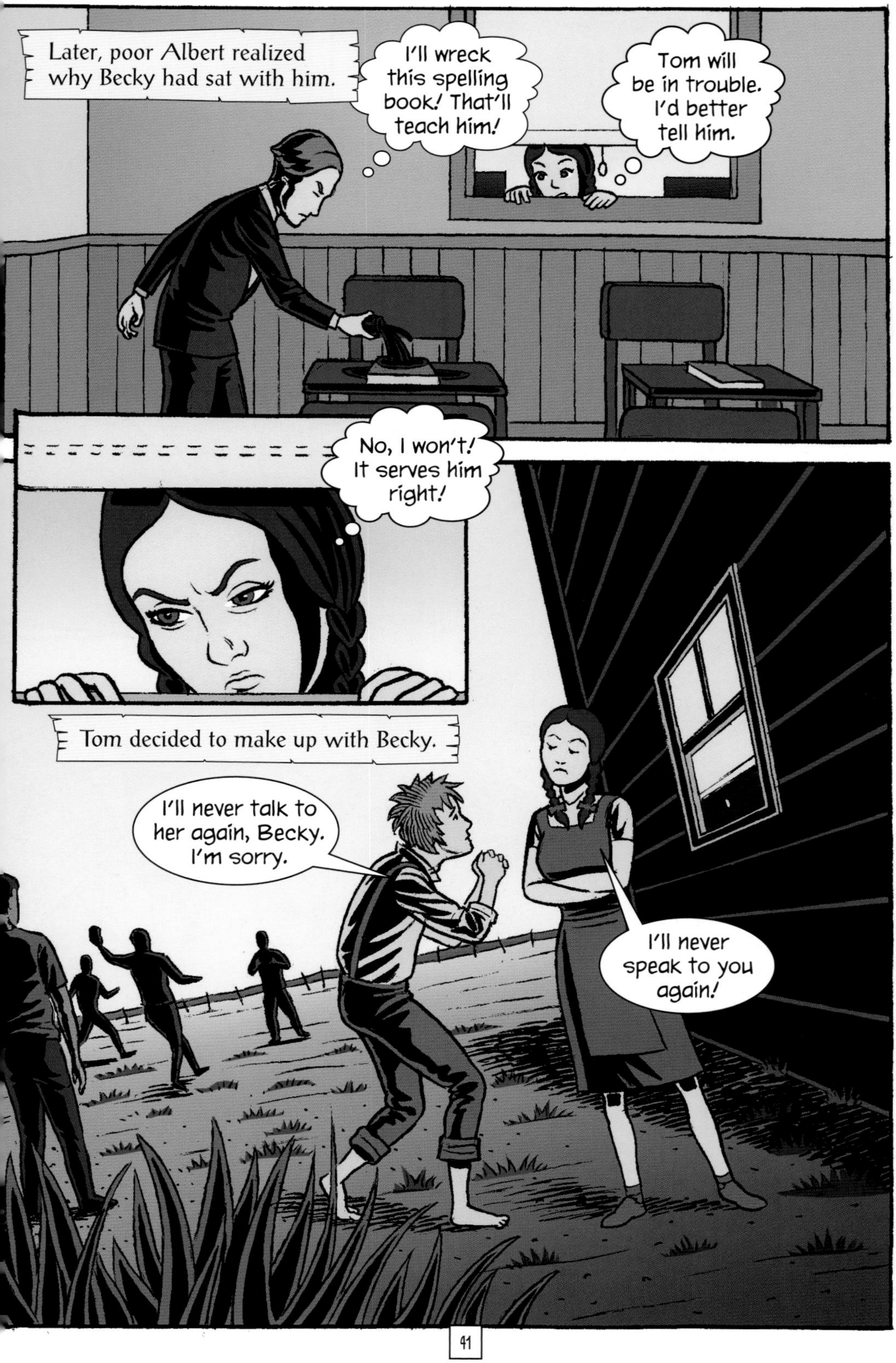
Later, poor Albert realized why Becky had sat with him.
I'll wreck this spelling book! That'll teach him!
Tom will be in trouble. I'd better tell him.
No, I won't! It serves him right!
Tom decided to make up with Becky.
I'll never talk to her again, Becky. I'm sorry.
I'll never speak to you again!

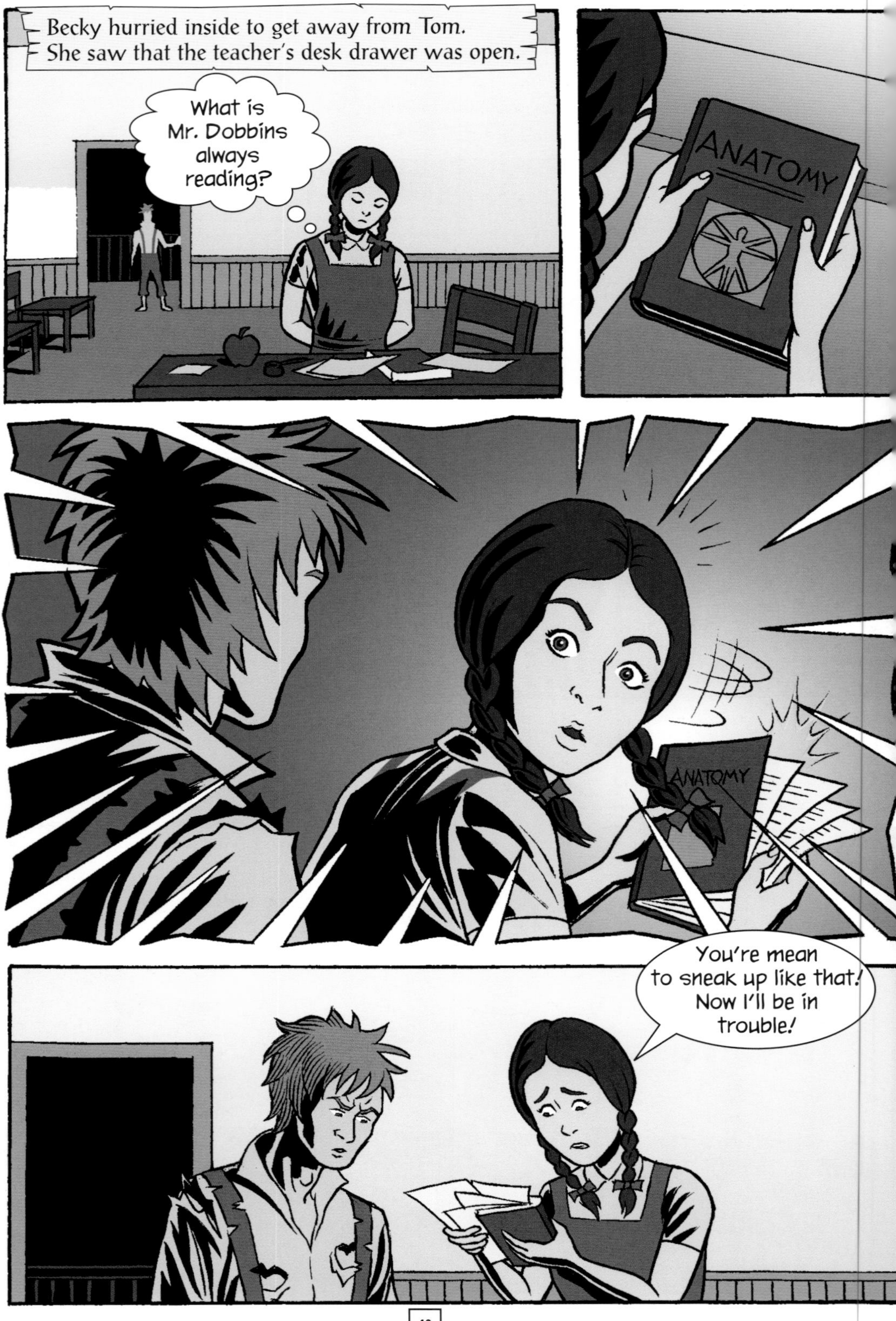
Becky hurried inside to get away from Tom. She saw that the teacher's desk drawer was open.
What is Mr. Dobbins always reading?
ANATOMY
ANATOMY
You're mean to sneak up like that! Now I'll be in trouble!

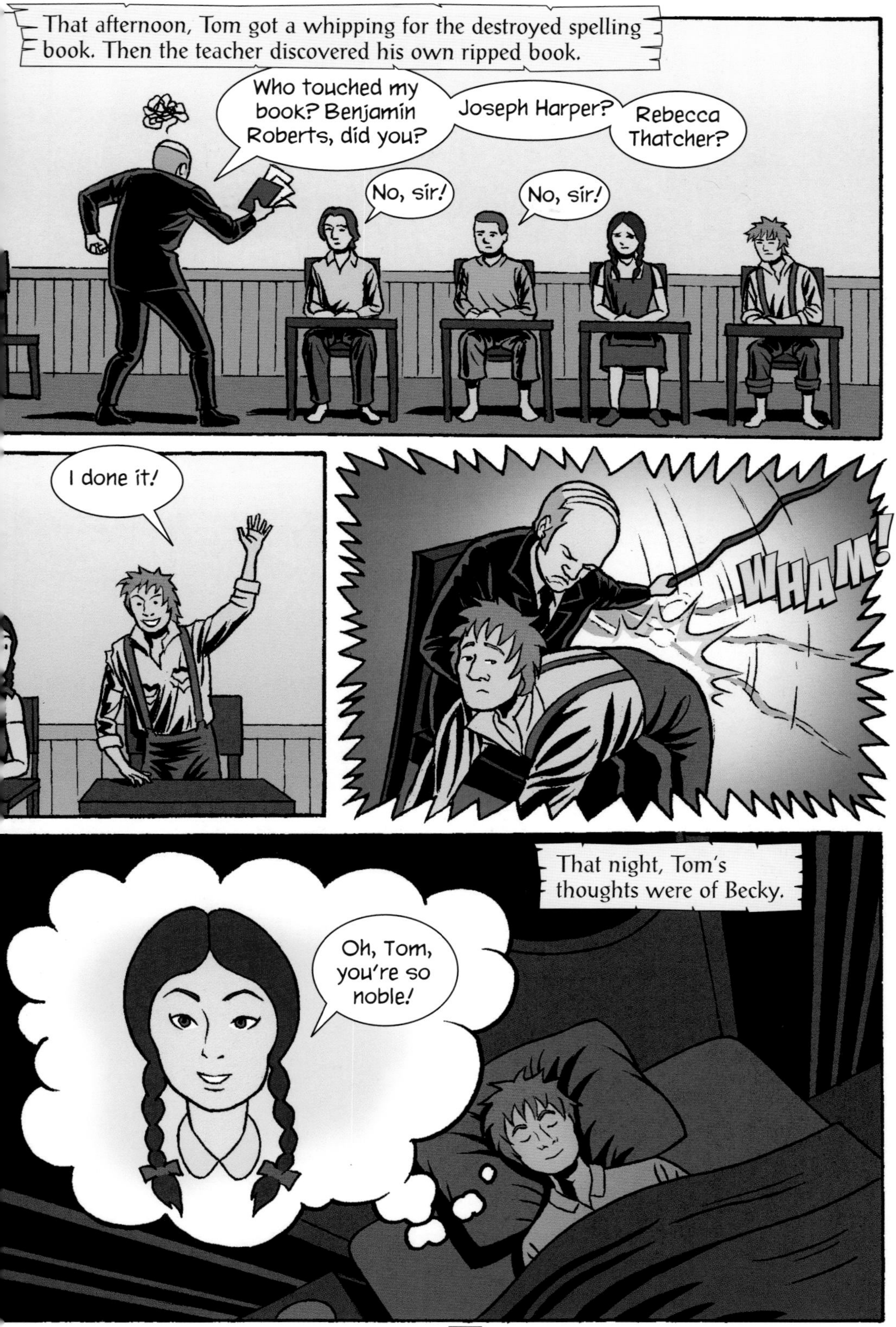
That afternoon, Tom got a whipping for the destroyed spelling book. Then the teacher discovered his own ripped book.
Who touched my book? Benjamin Roberts, did you?
No, sir!
Joseph Harper?
No, sir!
Rebecca Thatcher?
I done it!
WHAM!
That night, Tom's thoughts were of Becky.
Oh, Tom, you're so noble!

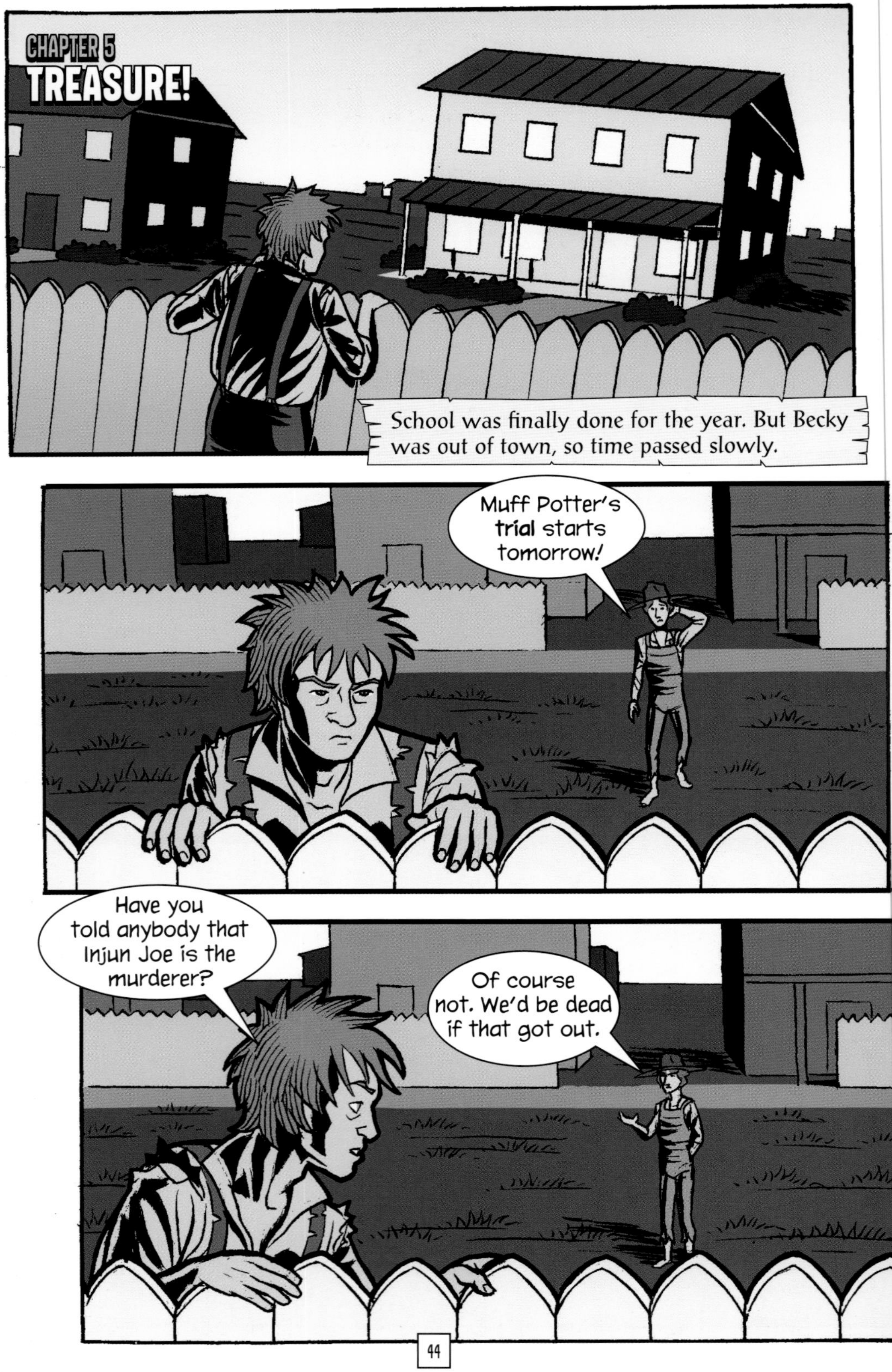
CHAPTER 5
TREASURE!
School was finally done for the year. But Becky was out of town, so time passed slowly.
Muff Potter's **trial** starts tomorrow!
Have you told anybody that Injun Joe is the murderer?
Of course not. We'd be dead if that got out.

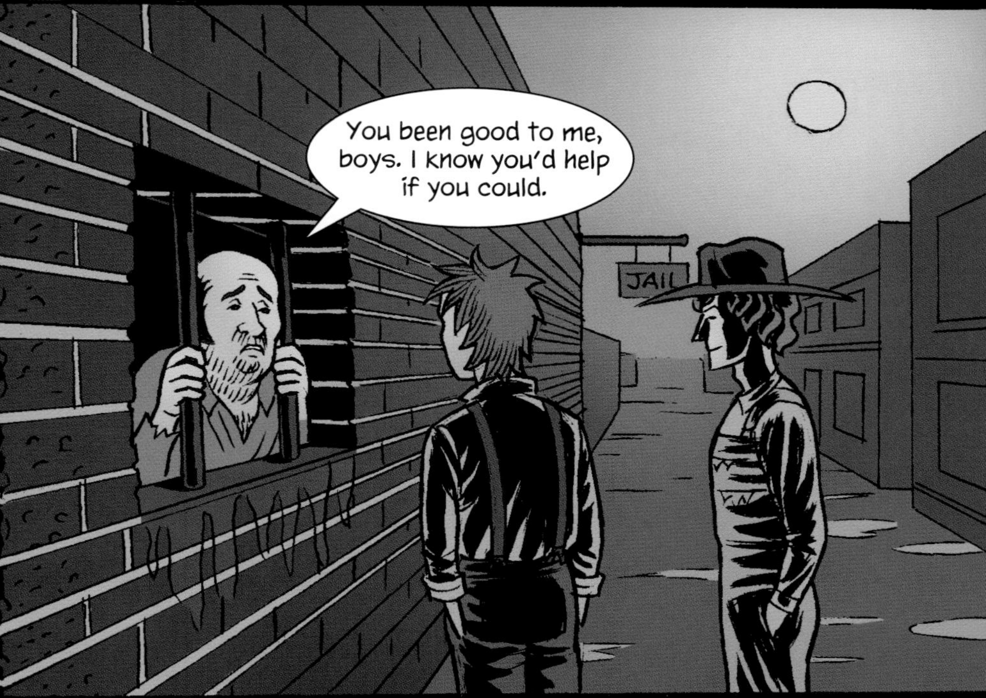
You been good to me, boys. I know you'd help if you could.
JAIL

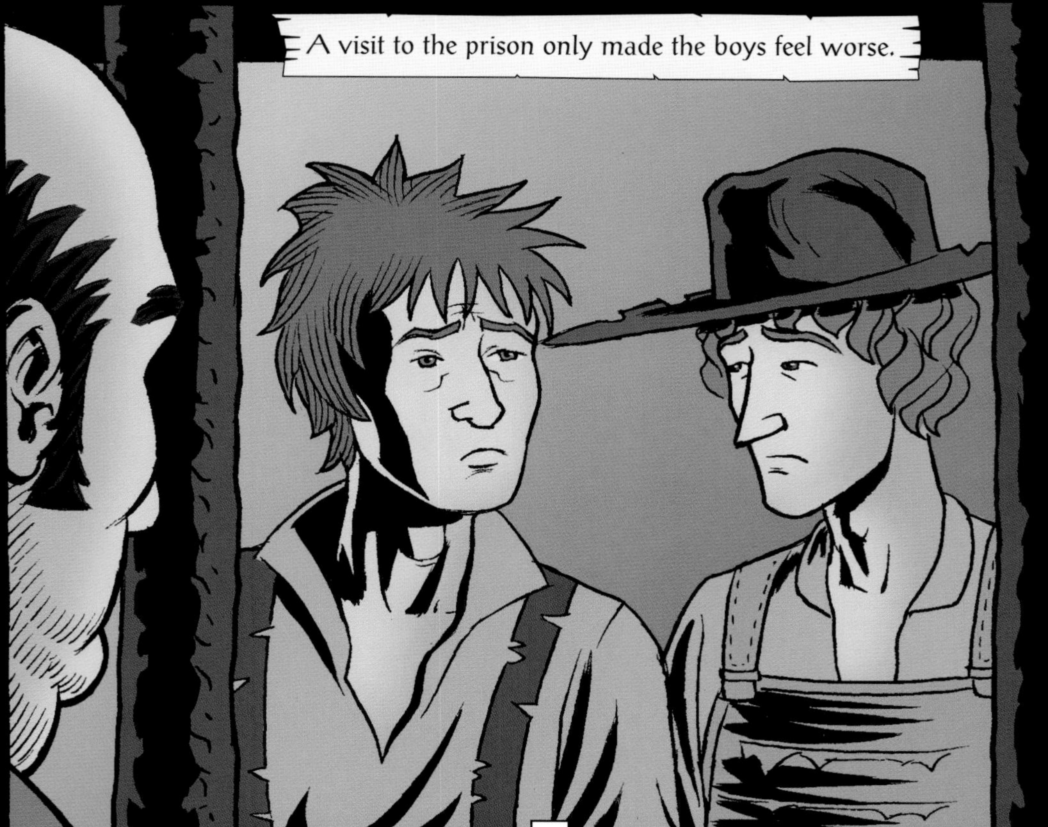
A visit to the prison only made the boys feel worse.

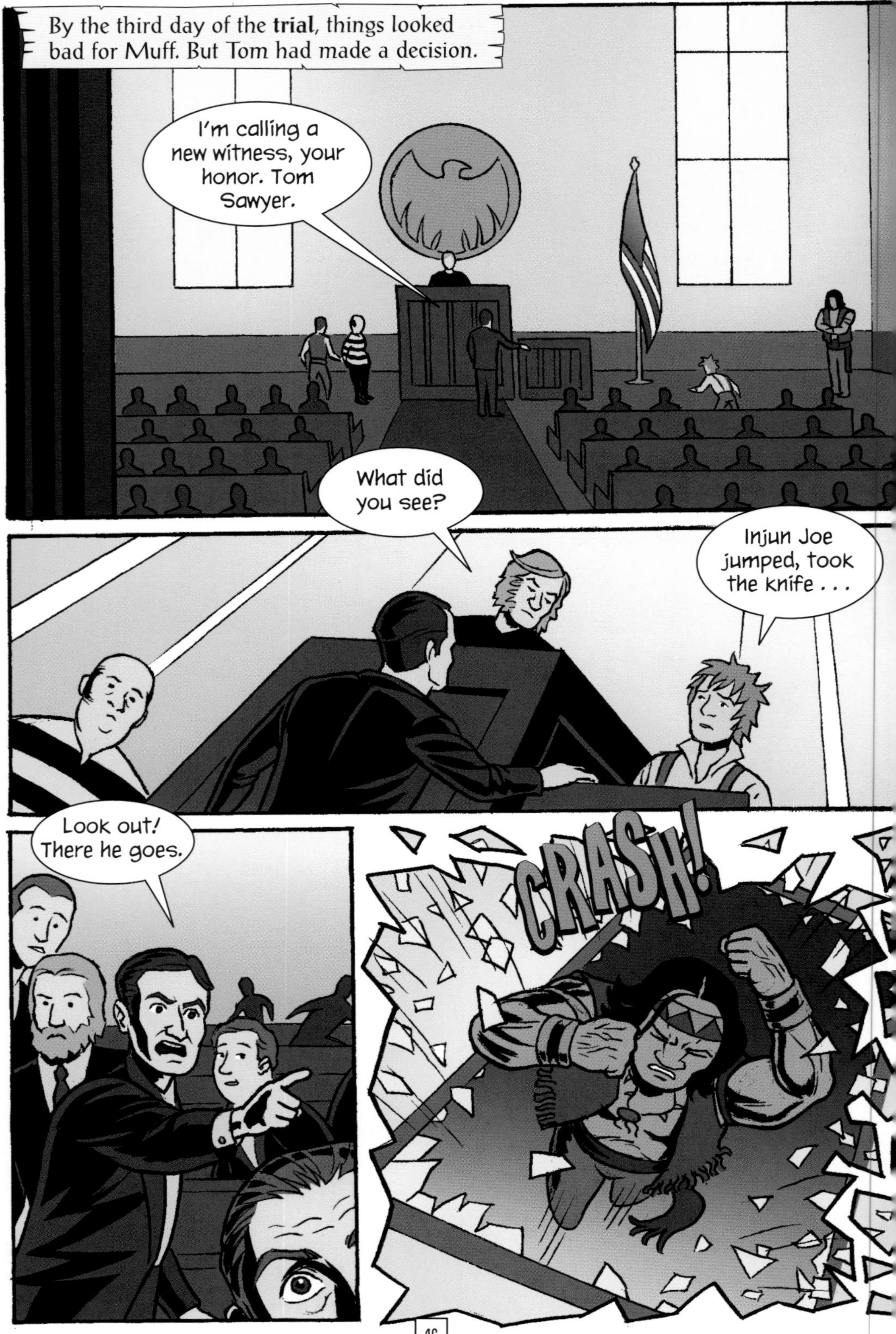
By the third day of the **trial**, things looked bad for Muff. But Tom had made a decision.
I'm calling a new witness, your honor. Tom Sawyer.
What did you see?
Injun Joe jumped, took the knife . . .
Look out! There he goes.
CRASH!

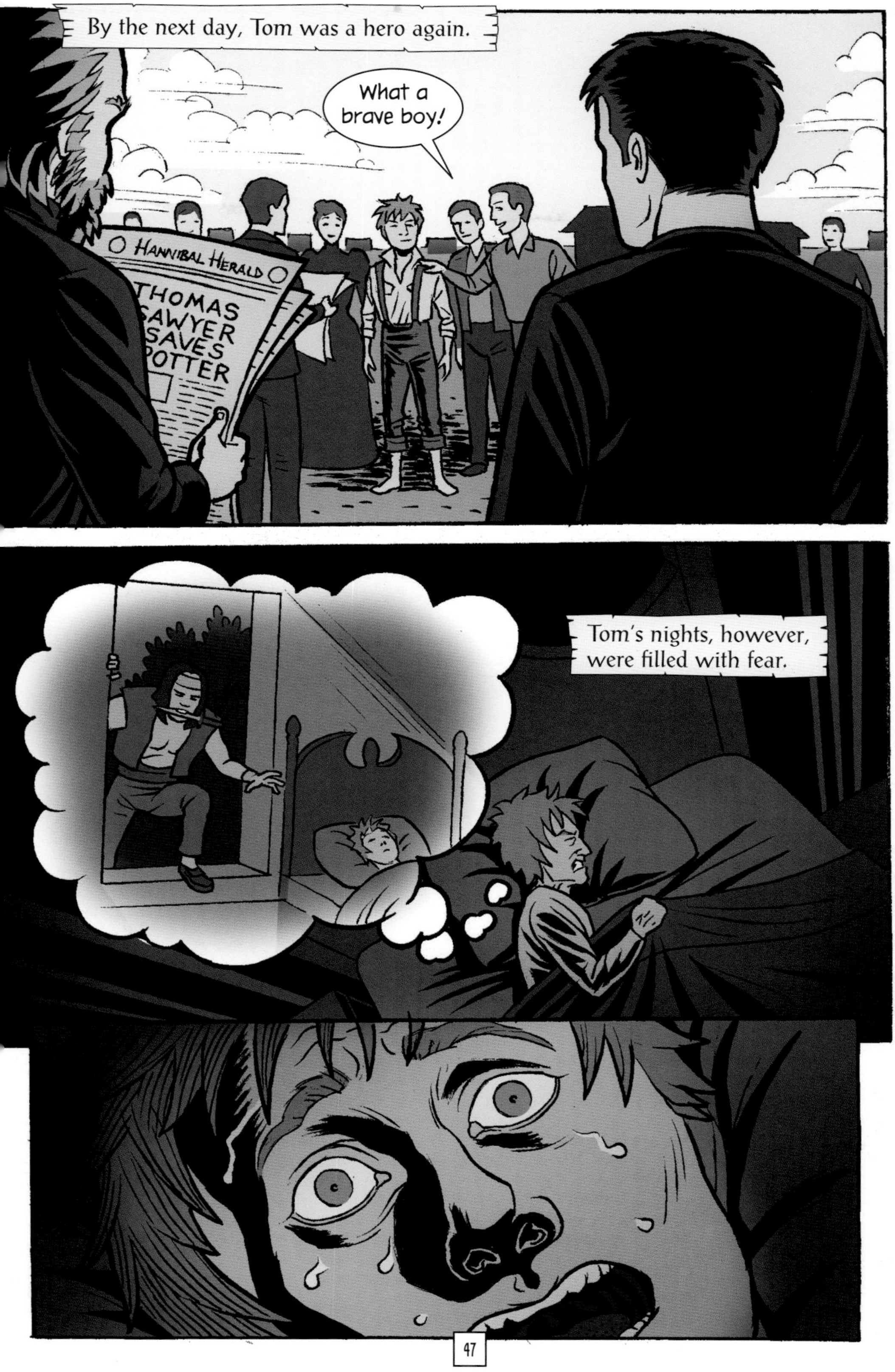
By the next day, Tom was a hero again.
What a brave boy!
HANNIBAL HERALD
THOMAS SAWYER SAVES POTTER
Tom's nights, however, were filled with fear.

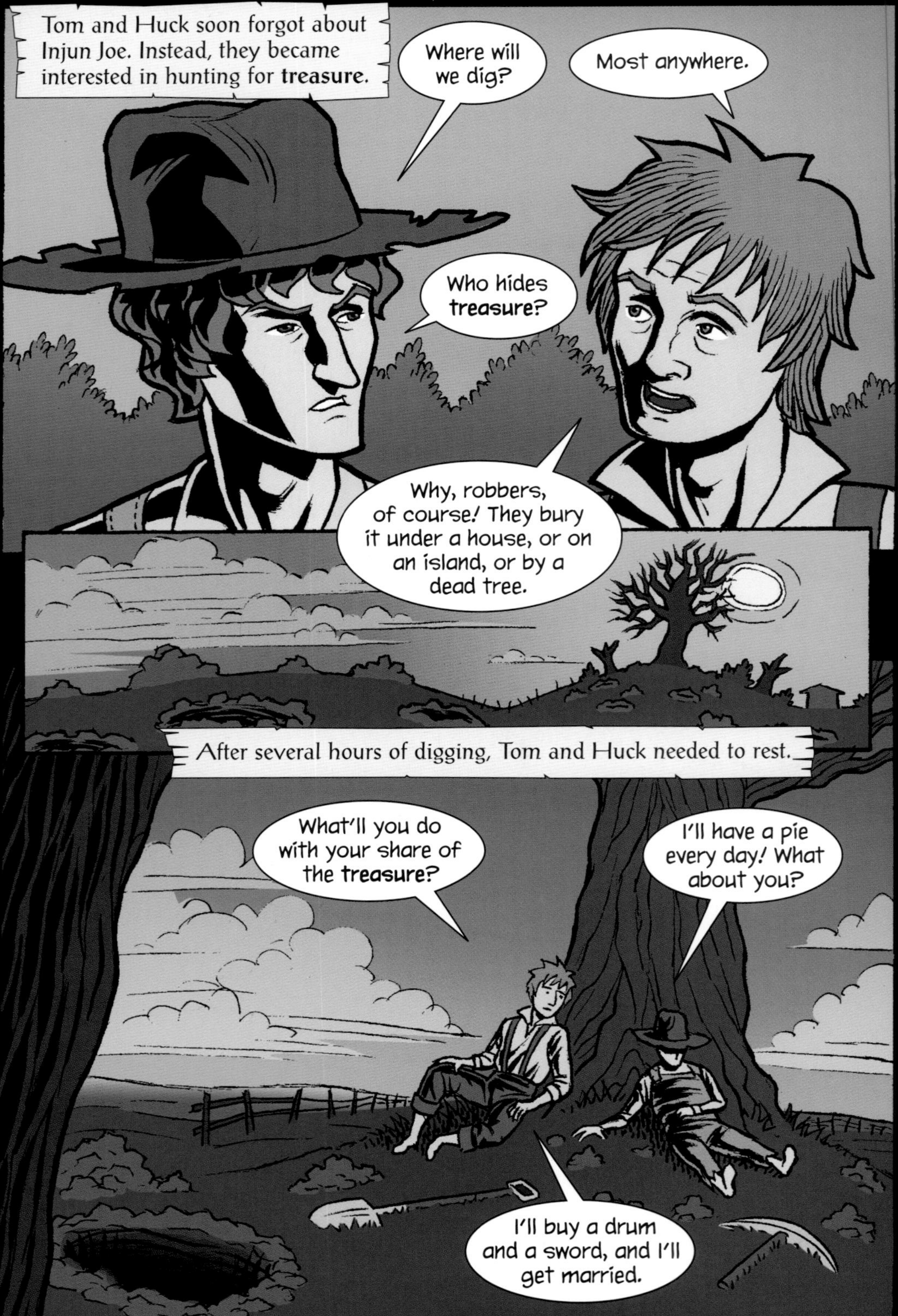

Tom and Huck soon forgot about Injun Joe. Instead, they became interested in hunting for treasure.
Where will we dig?
Most anywhere.
Who hides treasure?
Why, robbers, of course! They bury it under a house, or on an island, or by a dead tree.
After several hours of digging, Tom and Huck needed to rest.
What'll you do with your share of the treasure?
I'll have a pie every day! What about you?
I'll buy a drum and a sword, and I'll get married.

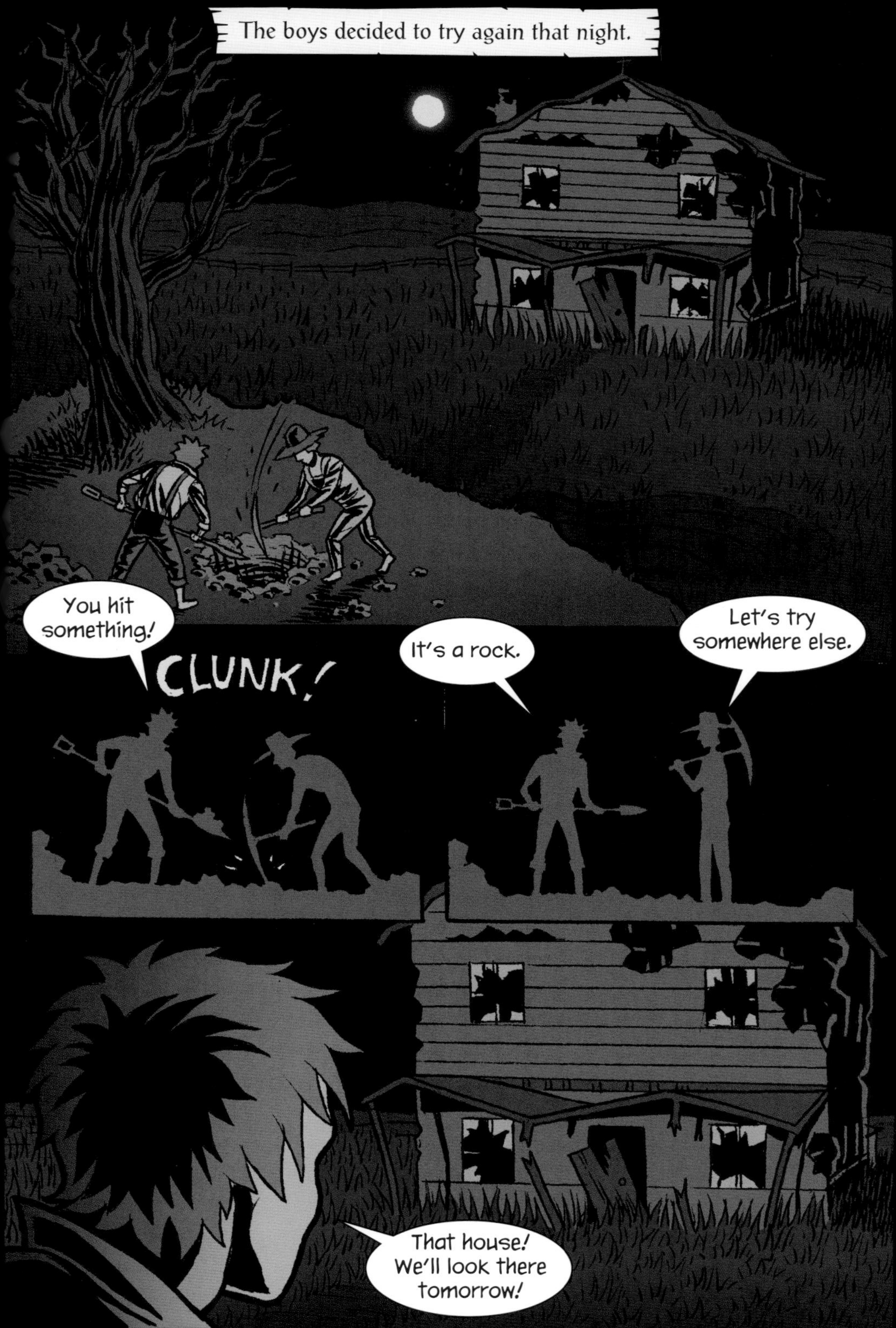
The boys decided to try again that night.
You hit something!
CLUNK!
It's a rock.
Let's try somewhere else.
That house! We'll look there tomorrow!

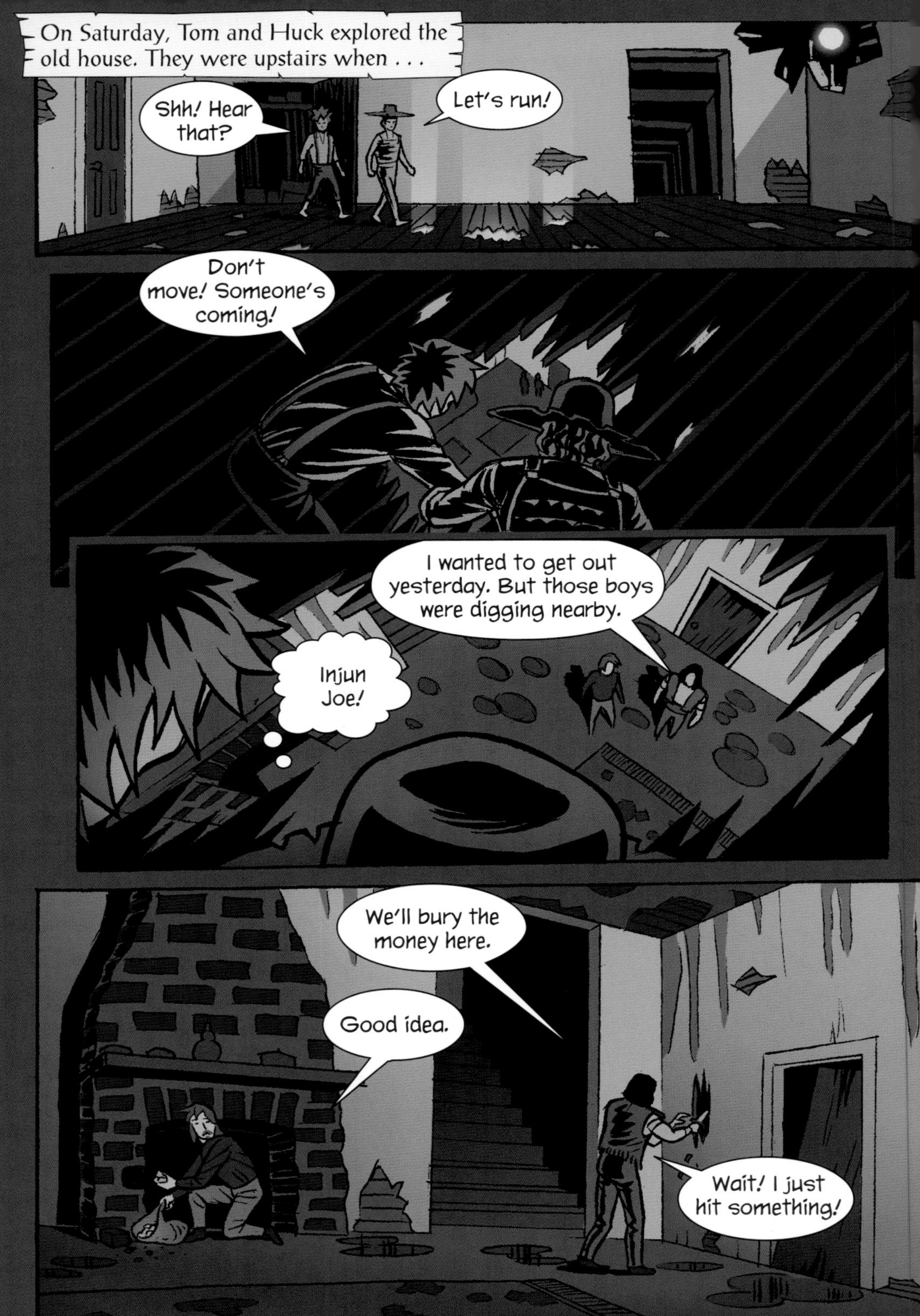
On Saturday, Tom and Huck explored the old house. They were upstairs when . . .
Shh! Hear that?
Let's run!
Don't move! Someone's coming!
I wanted to get out yesterday. But those boys were digging nearby.
Injun Joe!
We'll bury the money here.
Good idea.
Wait! I just hit something!

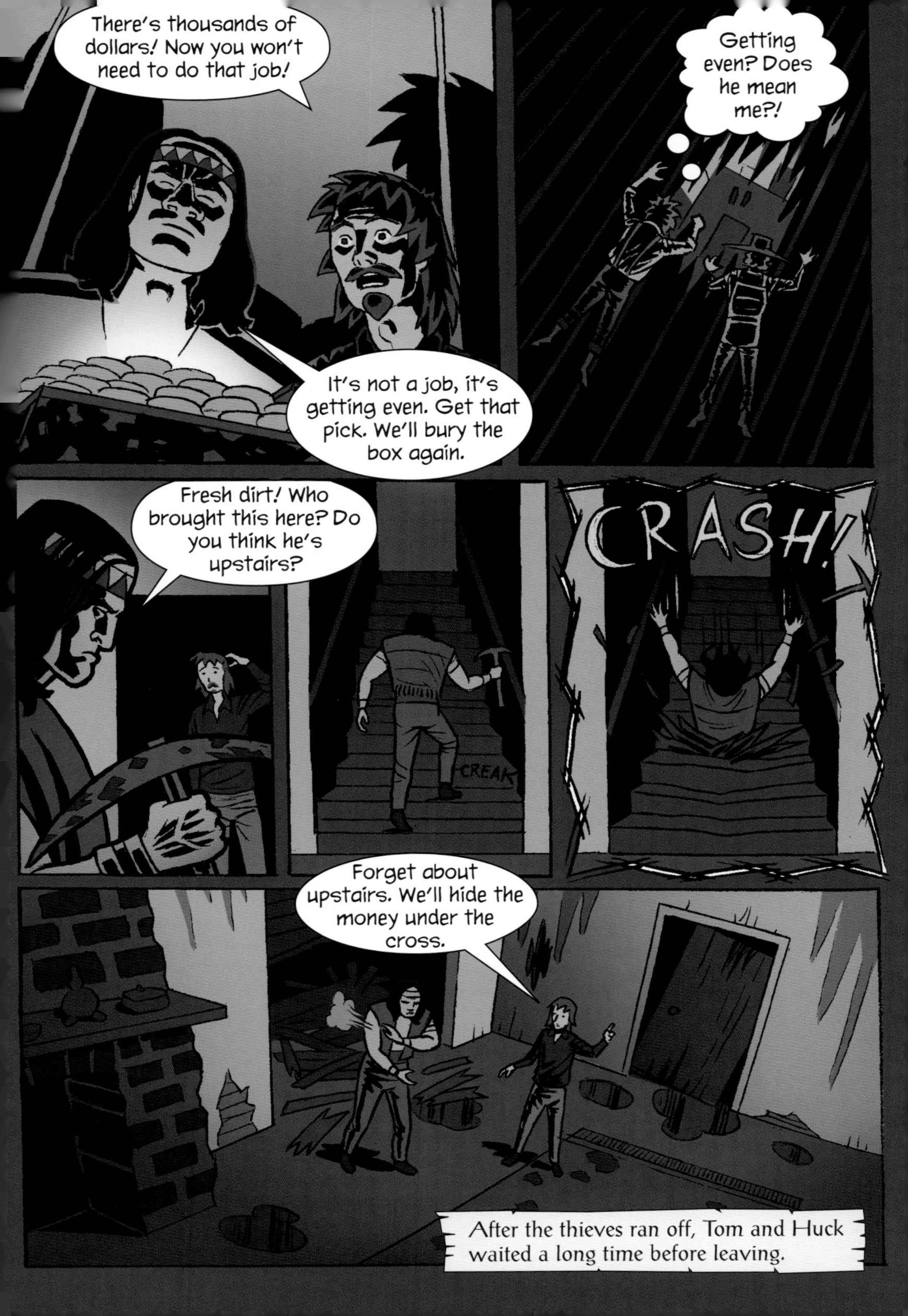
There's thousands of dollars! Now you won't need to do that job!
It's not a job, it's getting even. Get that pick. We'll bury the box again.
Getting even? Does he mean me?!
Fresh dirt! Who brought this here? Do you think he's upstairs?
CREAK
CRASH!
Forget about upstairs. We'll hide the money under the cross.
After the thieves ran off, Tom and Huck waited a long time before leaving.

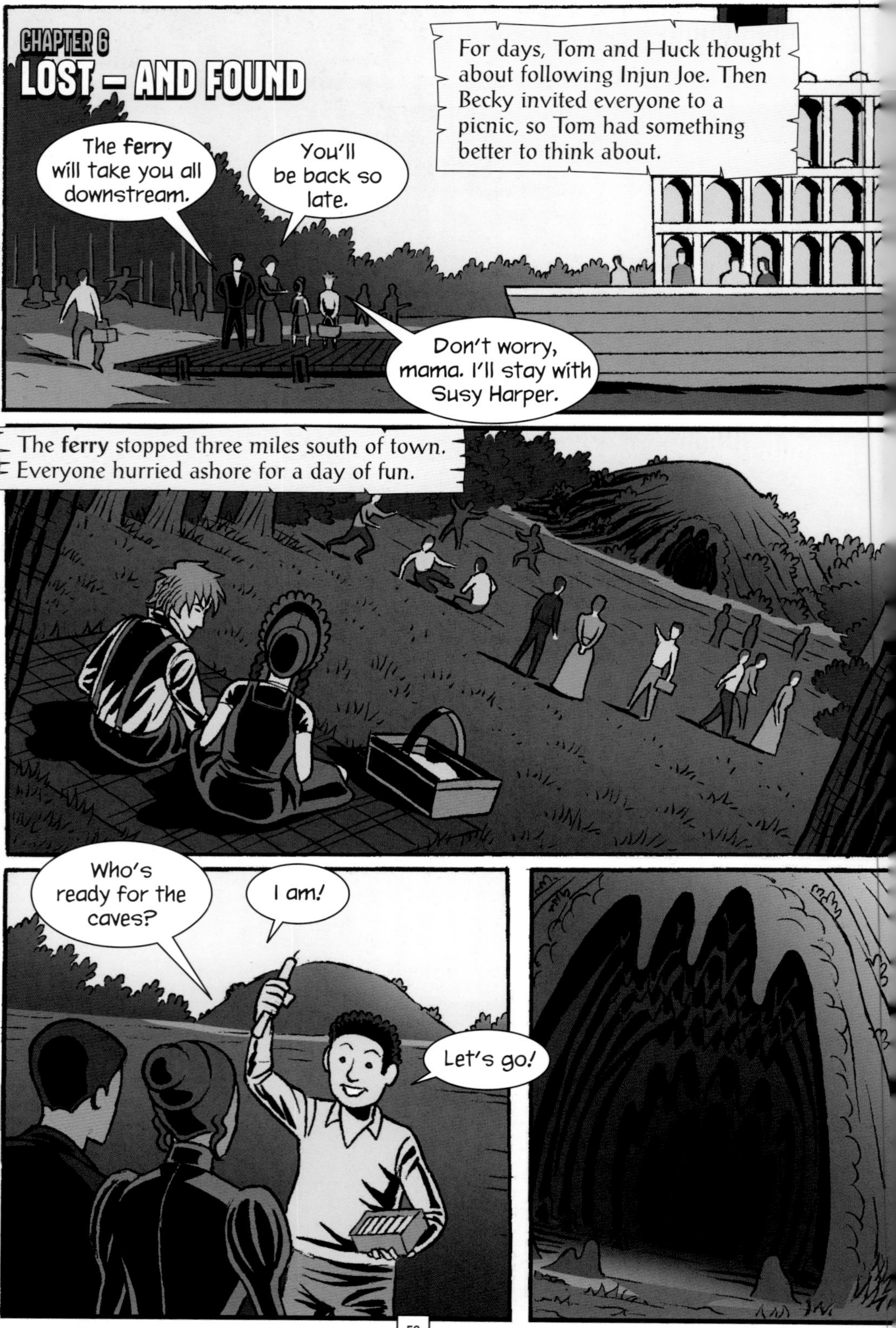
CHAPTER 6
LOST — AND FOUND
For days, Tom and Huck thought about following Injun Joe. Then Becky invited everyone to a picnic, so Tom had something better to think about.
The ferry will take you all downstream.
You'll be back so late.
Don't worry, mama. I'll stay with Susy Harper.
The ferry stopped three miles south of town. Everyone hurried ashore for a day of fun.
Who's ready for the caves?
I am!
Let's go!

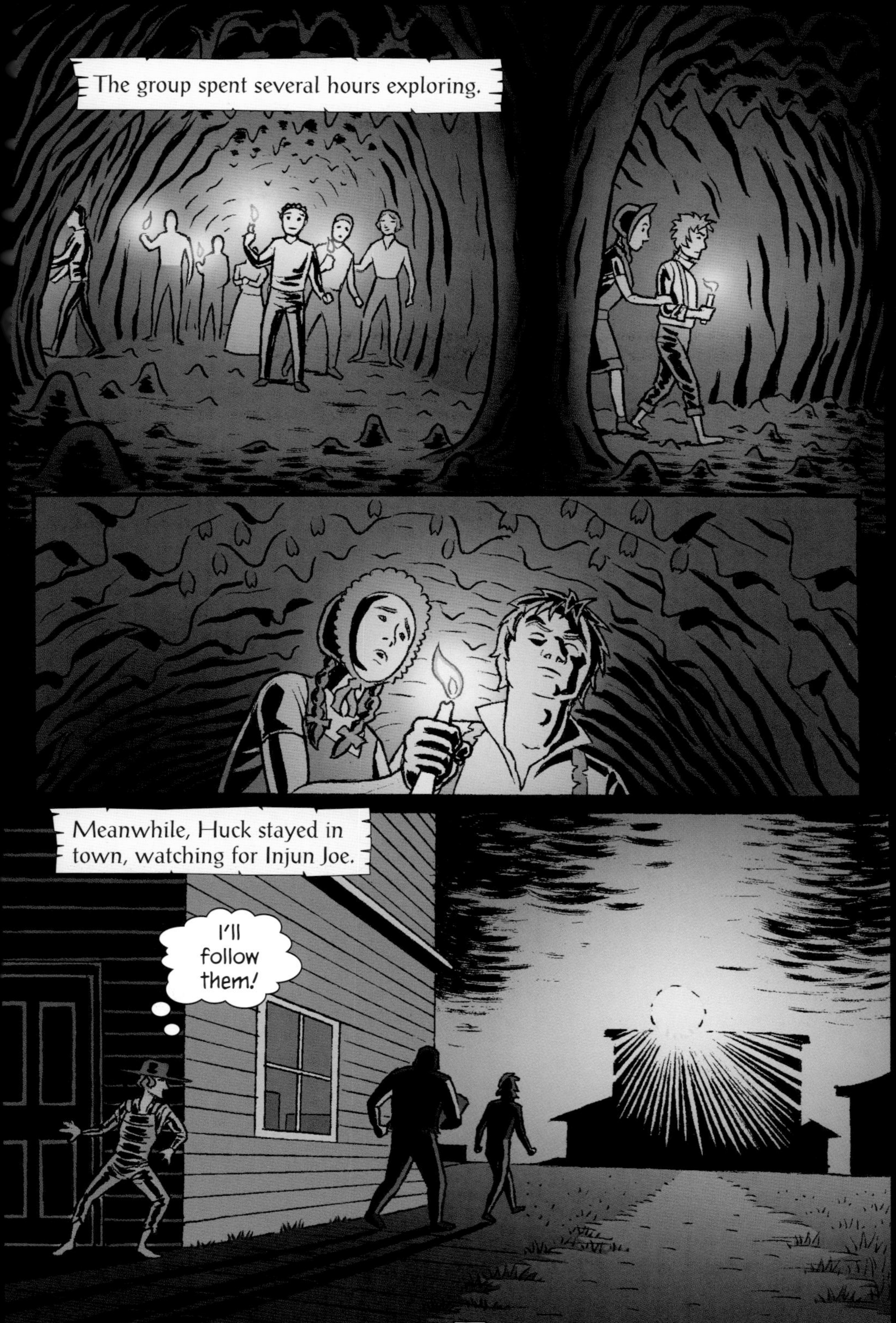
The group spent several hours exploring.
Meanwhile, Huck stayed in town, watching for Injun Joe.
I'll follow them!

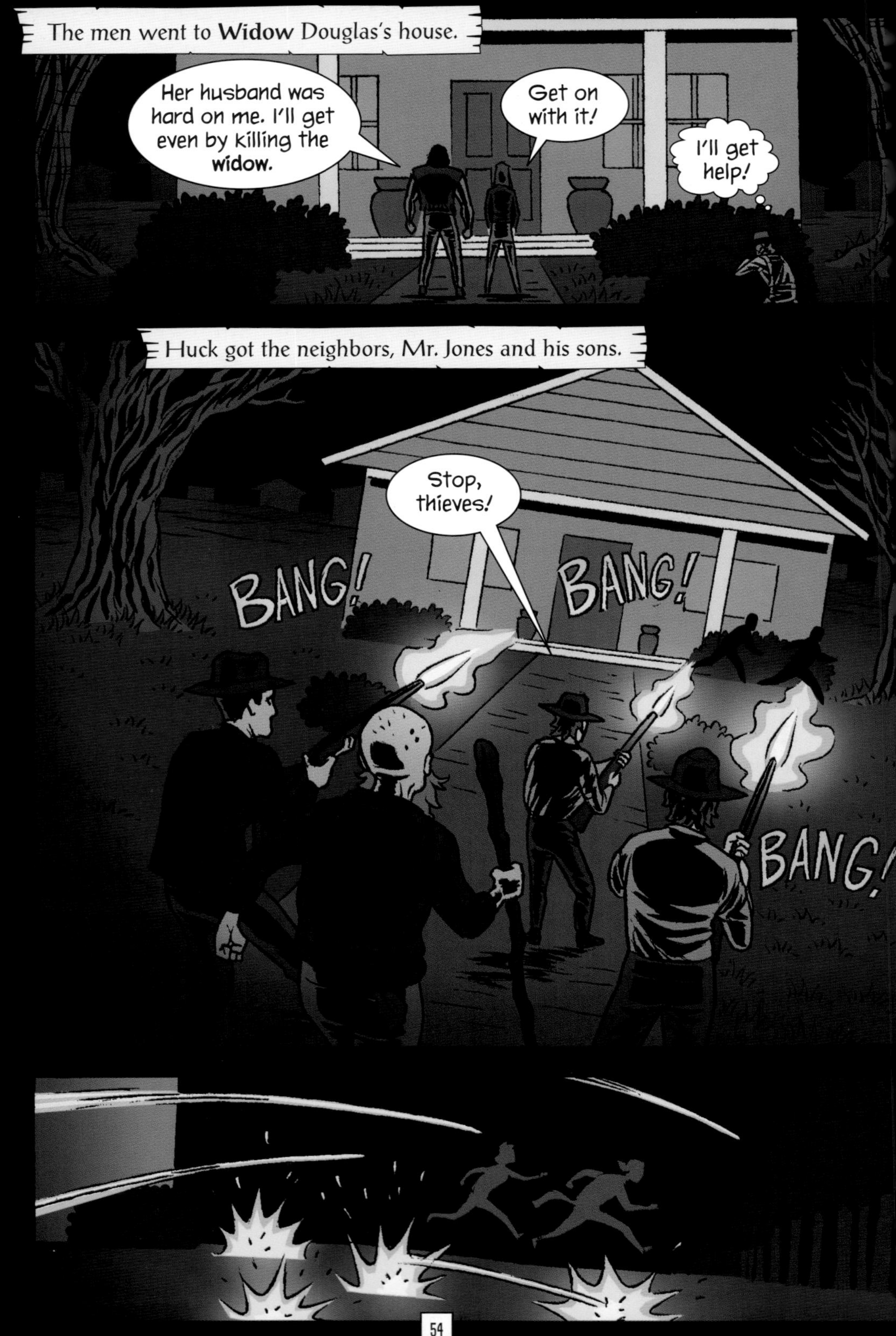
The men went to **Widow** Douglas's house.
Her husband was hard on me. I'll get even by killing the **widow.**
Get on with it!
I'll get help!
Huck got the neighbors, Mr. Jones and his sons.
Stop, thieves!
BANG!
BANG!
BANG!

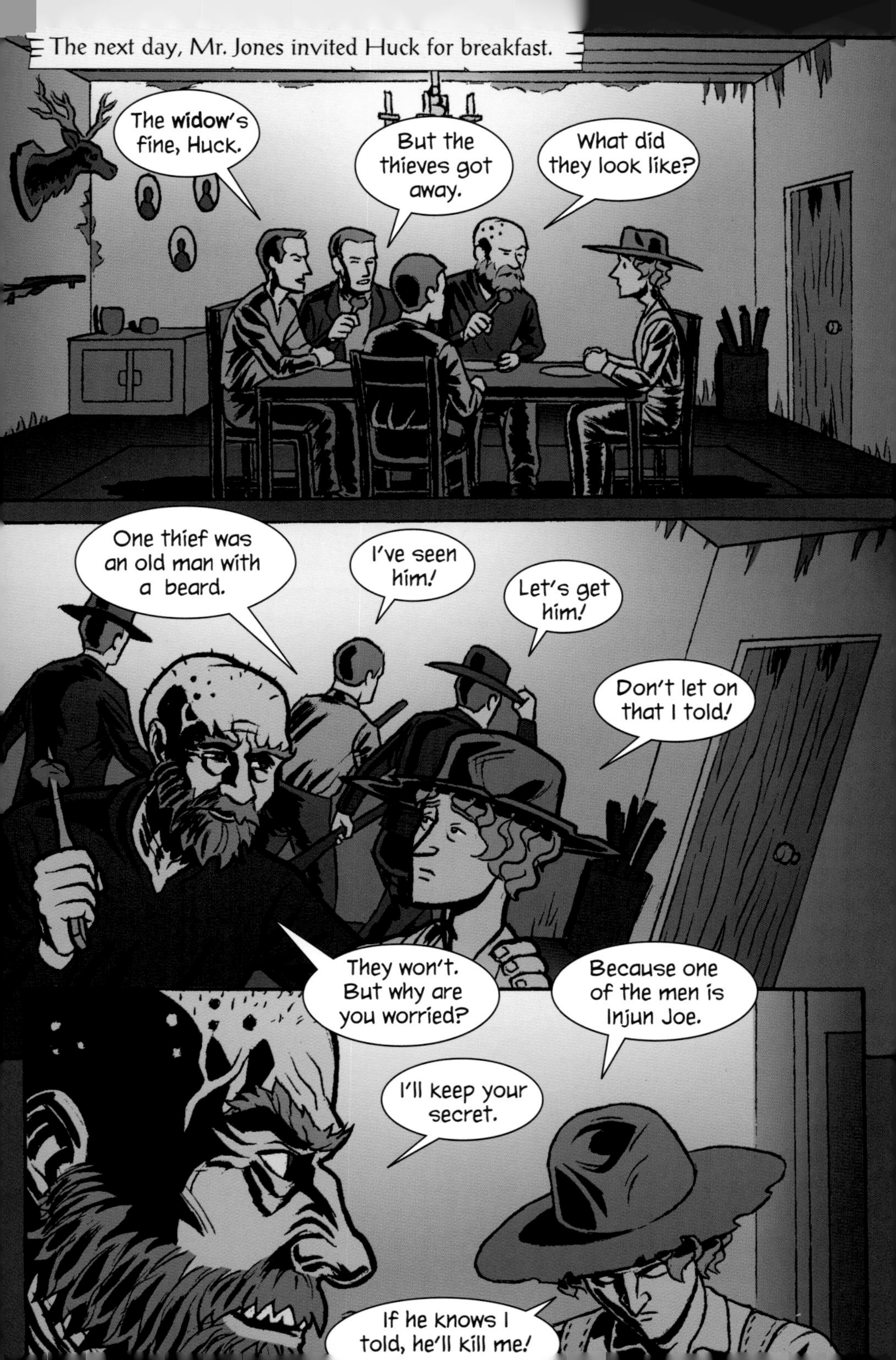
The next day, Mr. Jones invited Huck for breakfast.
The widow's fine, Huck.
But the thieves got away.
What did they look like?
One thief was an old man with a beard.
I've seen him!
Let's get him!
Don't let on that I told!
They won't. But why are you worried?
Because one of the men is Injun Joe.
I'll keep your secret.
If he knows I told, he'll kill me!

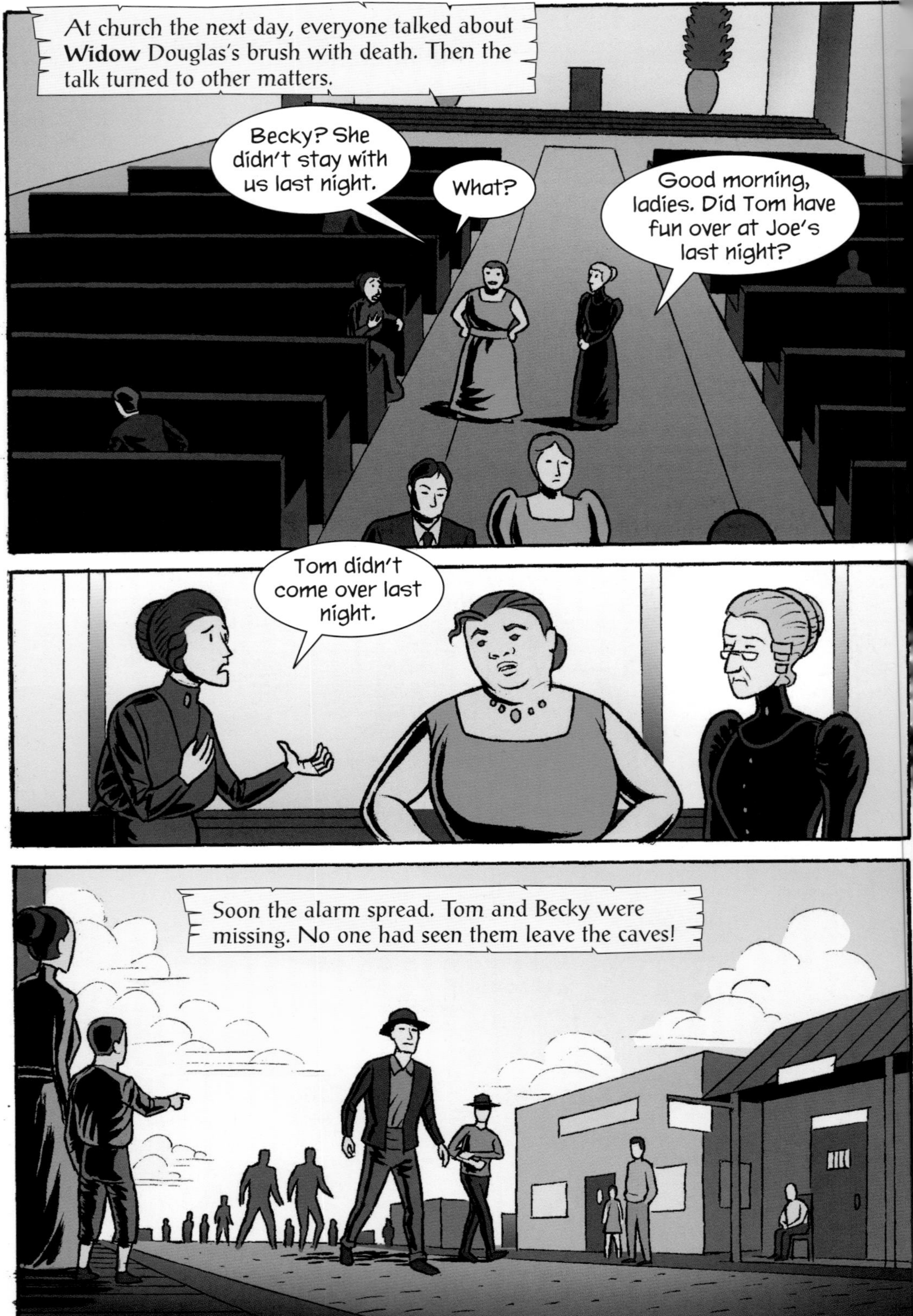
At church the next day, everyone talked about **Widow** Douglas's brush with death. Then the talk turned to other matters.
Becky? She didn't stay with us last night.
What?
Good morning, ladies. Did Tom have fun over at Joe's last night?
Tom didn't come over last night.
Soon the alarm spread. Tom and Becky were missing. No one had seen them leave the caves!

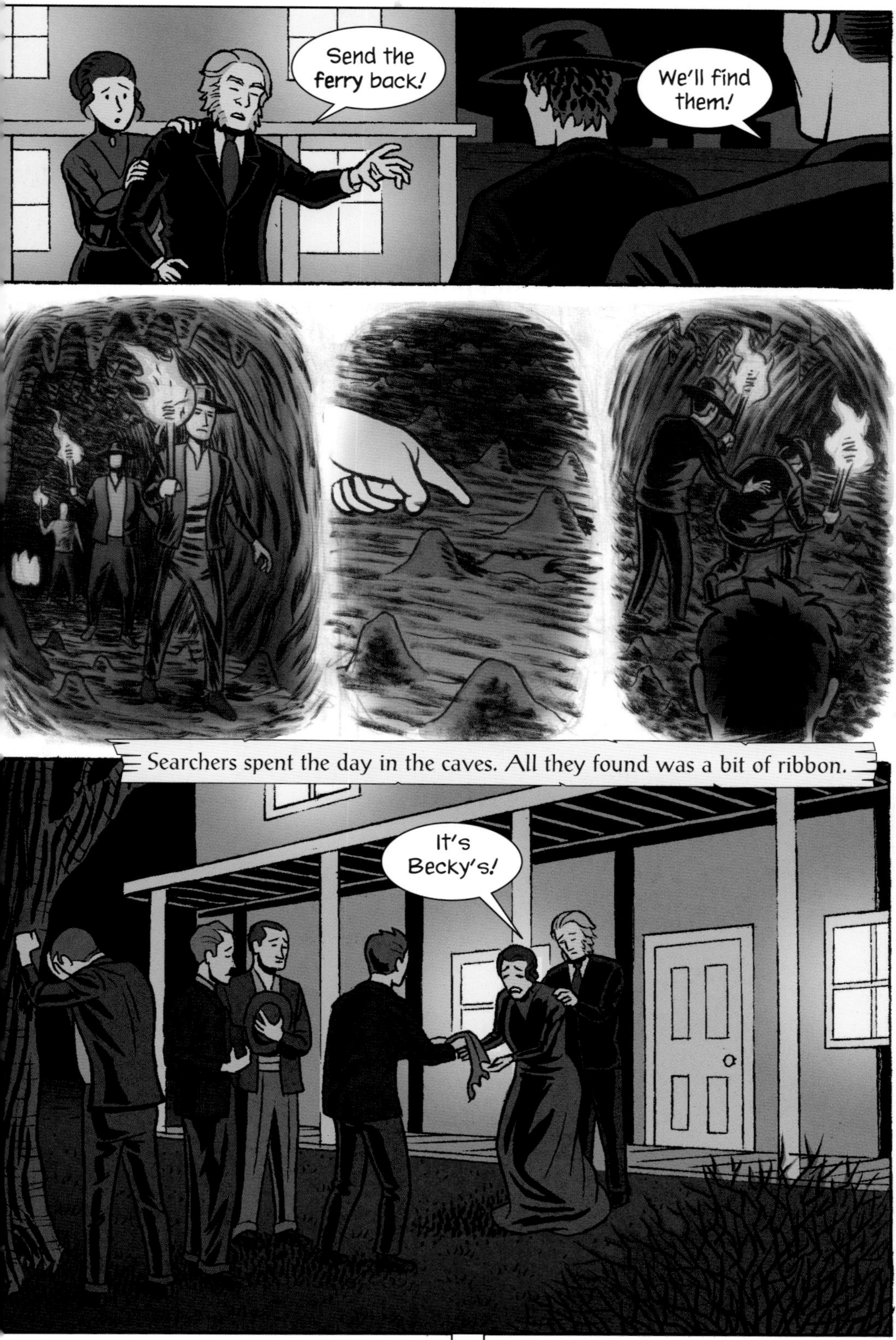
Send the ferry back!
We'll find them!
Searchers spent the day in the caves. All they found was a bit of ribbon.
It's Becky's!

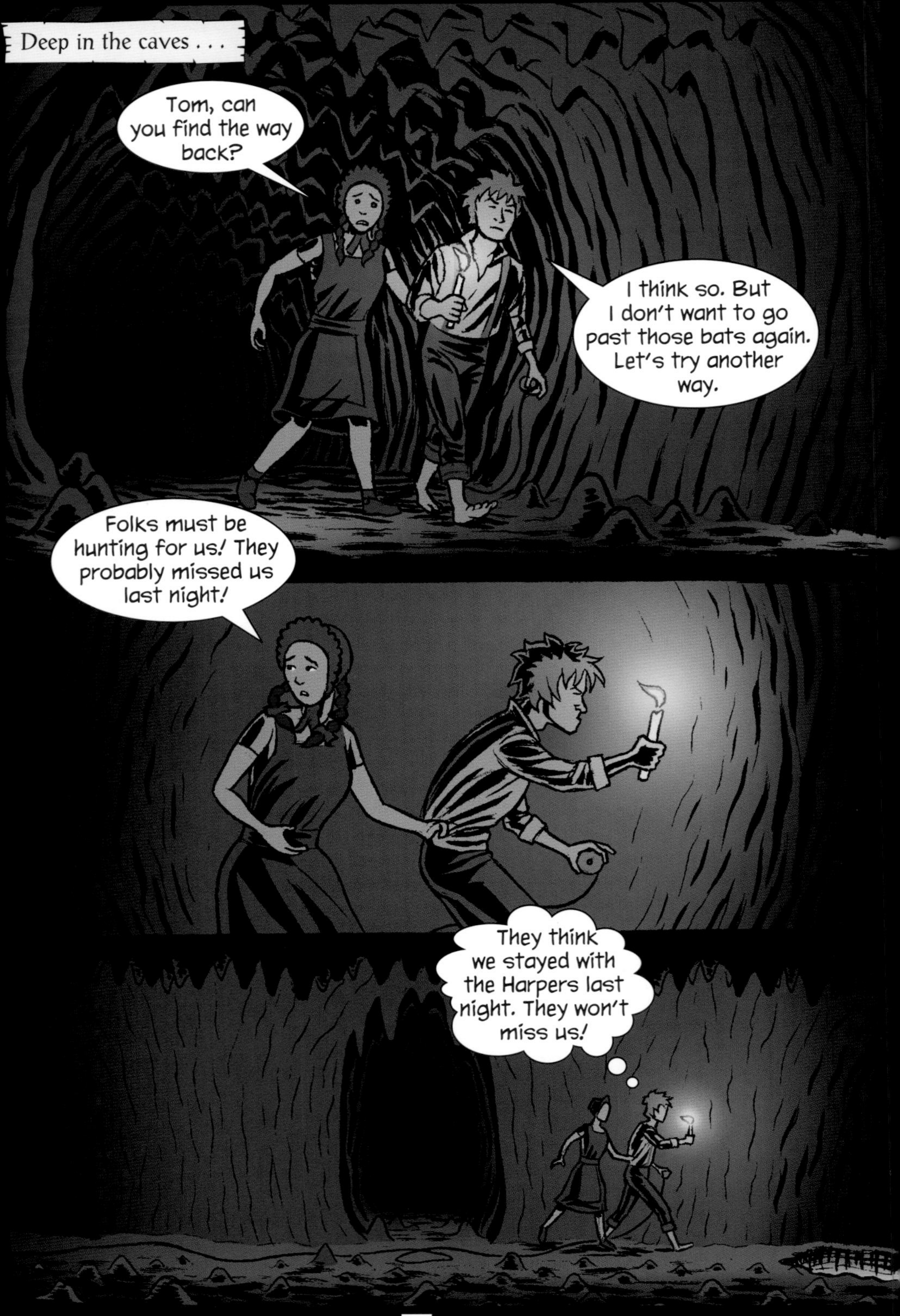
Deep in the caves . . .
Tom, can you find the way back?
I think so. But I don't want to go past those bats again. Let's try another way.
Folks must be hunting for us! They probably missed us last night!
They think we stayed with the Harpers last night. They won't miss us!

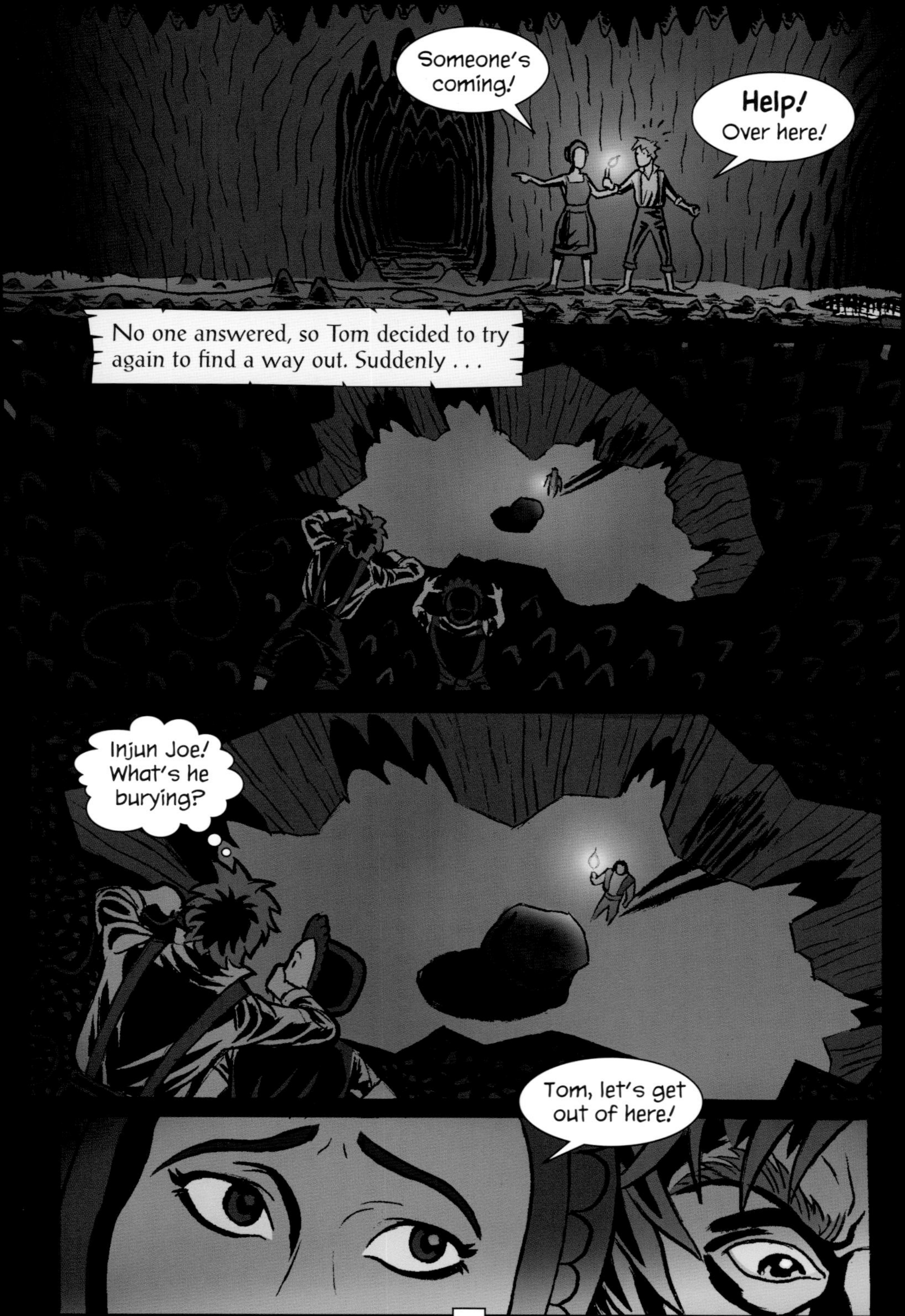

Someone's coming!
Help! Over here!
No one answered, so Tom decided to try again to find a way out. Suddenly . . .
Injun Joe! What's he burying?
Tom, let's get out of here!

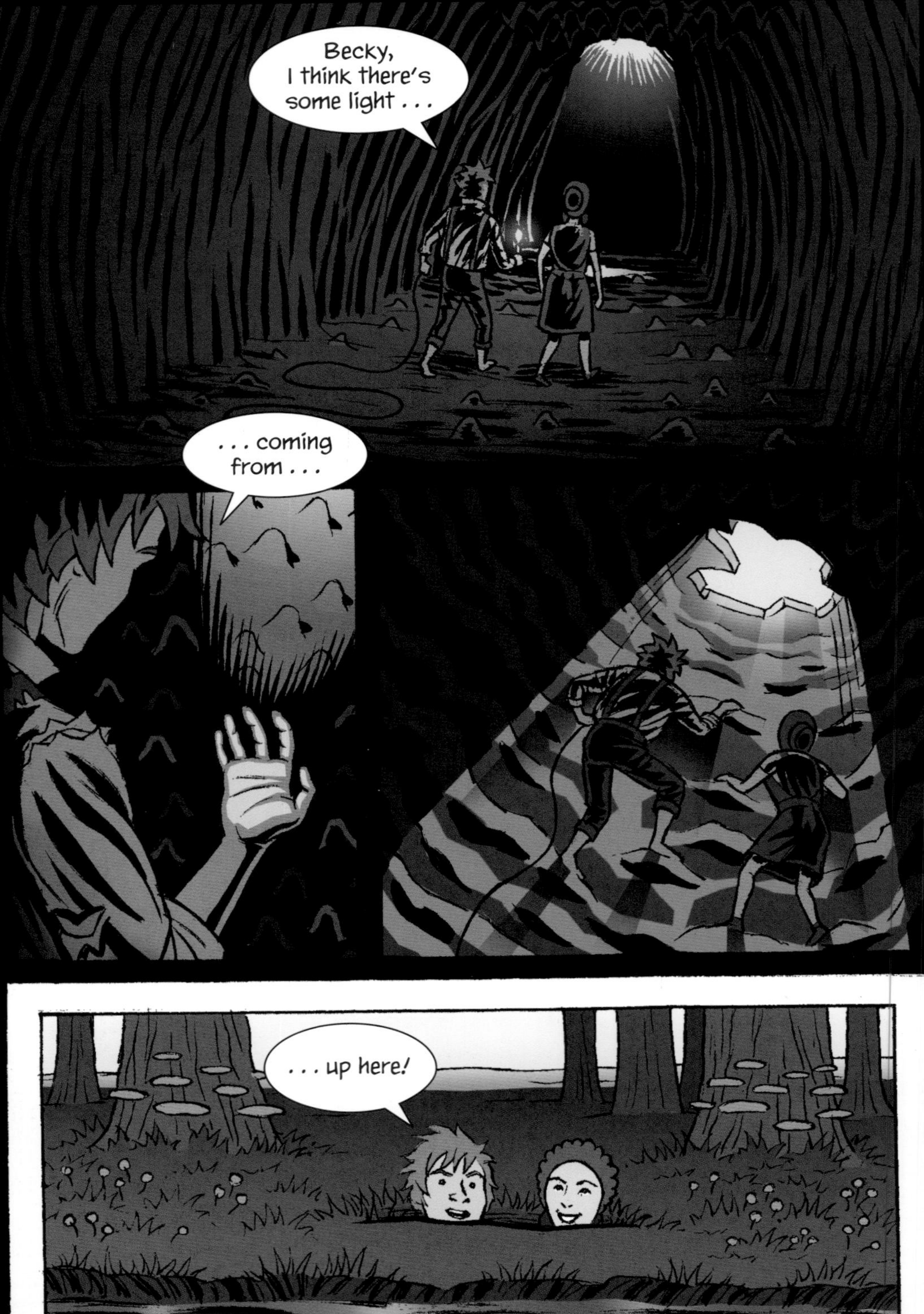
Becky, I think there's some light . . .
. . . coming from . . .
. . . up here!

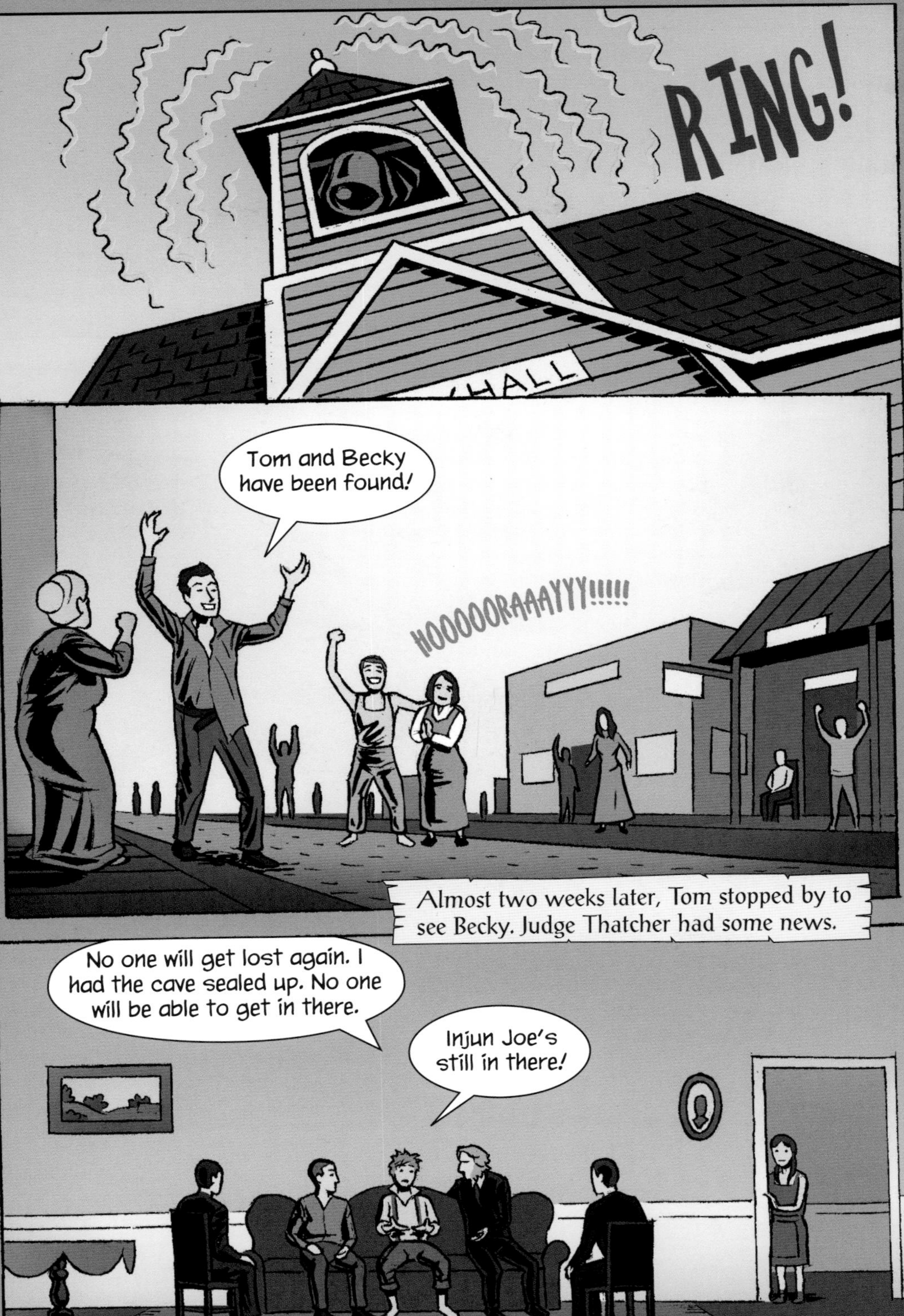

RING!
HALL
Tom and Becky have been found!
HOOOOORAAAYYY!!!!!
Almost two weeks later, Tom stopped by to see Becky. Judge Thatcher had some news.
No one will get lost again. I had the cave sealed up. No one will be able to get in there.
Injun Joe's still in there!

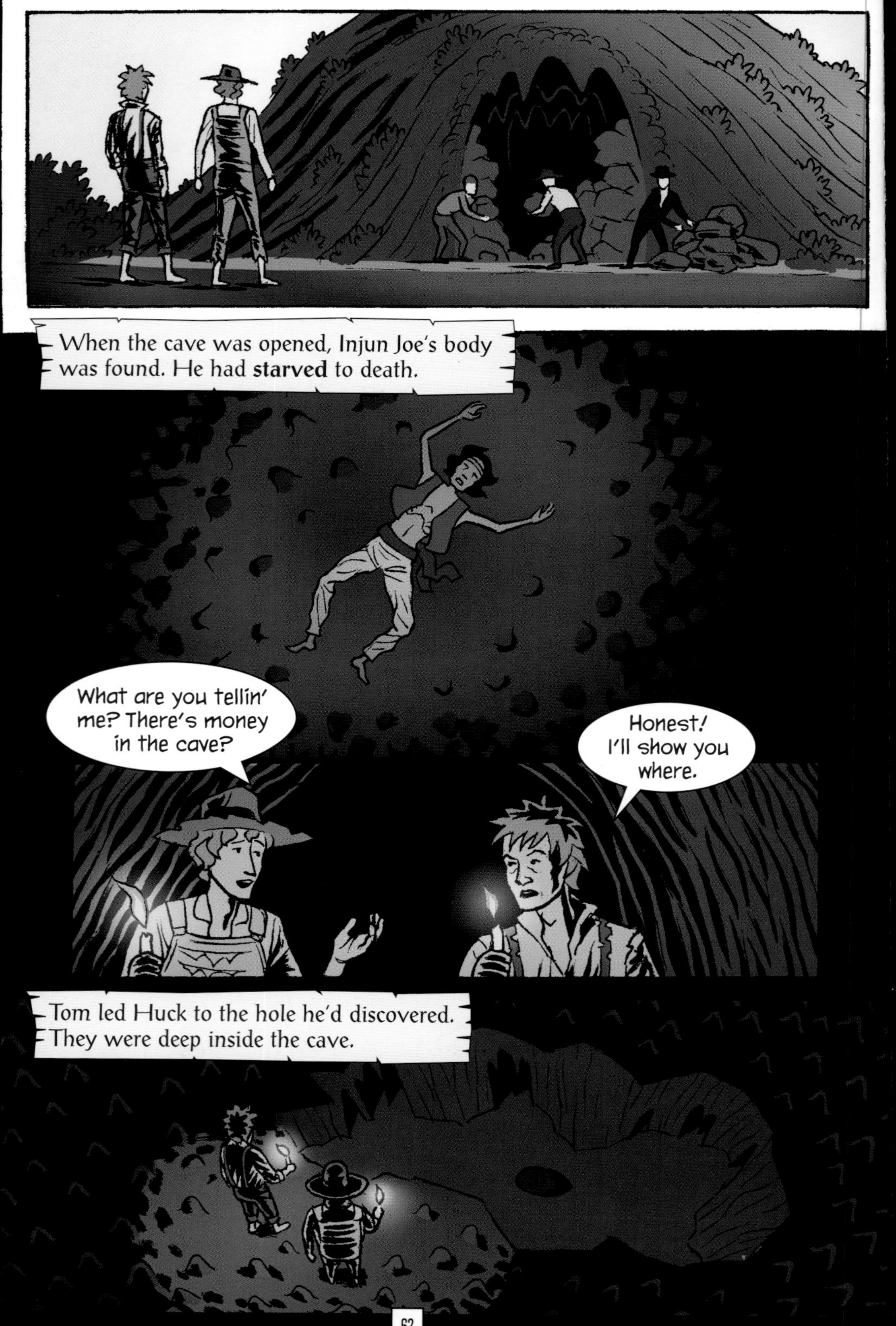

When the cave was opened, Injun Joe's body was found. He had **starved** to death.
What are you tellin' me? There's money in the cave?
Honest! I'll show you where.
Tom led Huck to the hole he'd discovered. They were deep inside the cave.

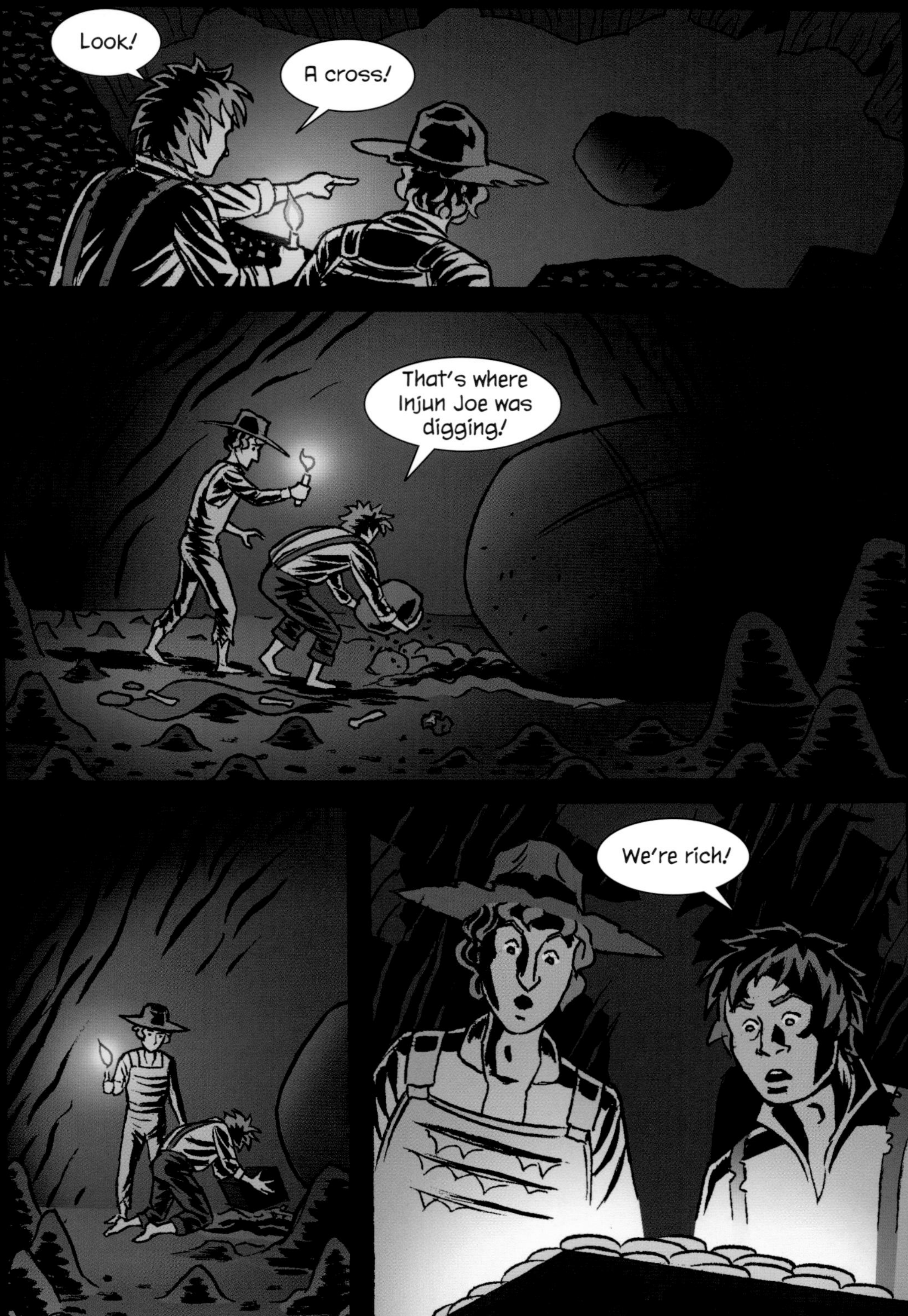
Look!
A cross!
That's where Injun Joe was digging!
We're rich!

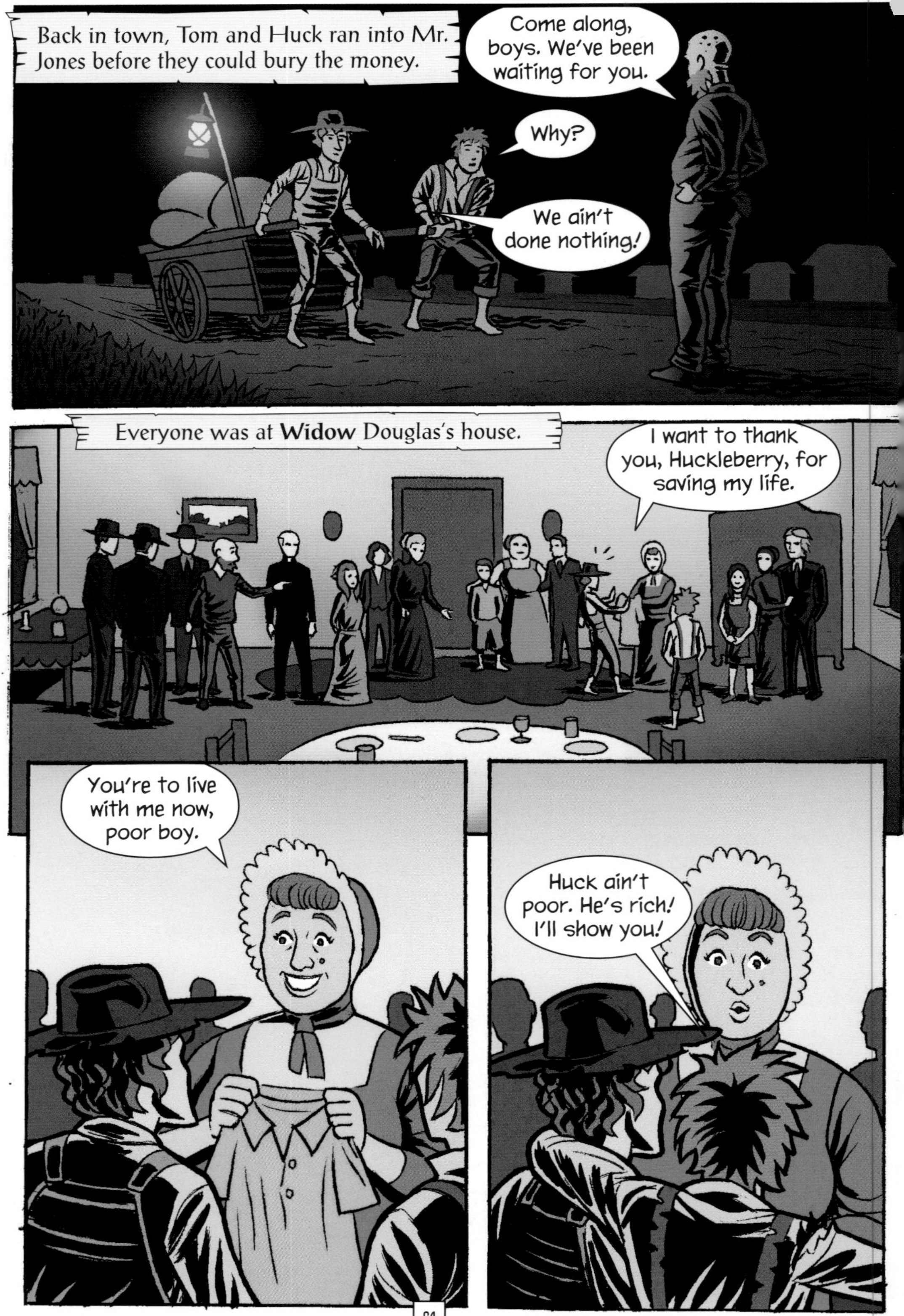
Back in town, Tom and Huck ran into Mr. Jones before they could bury the money.
Come along, boys. We've been waiting for you.
Why?
We ain't done nothing!
Everyone was at **Widow** Douglas's house.
I want to thank you, Huckleberry, for saving my life.
You're to live with me now, poor boy.
Huck ain't poor. He's rich! I'll show you!

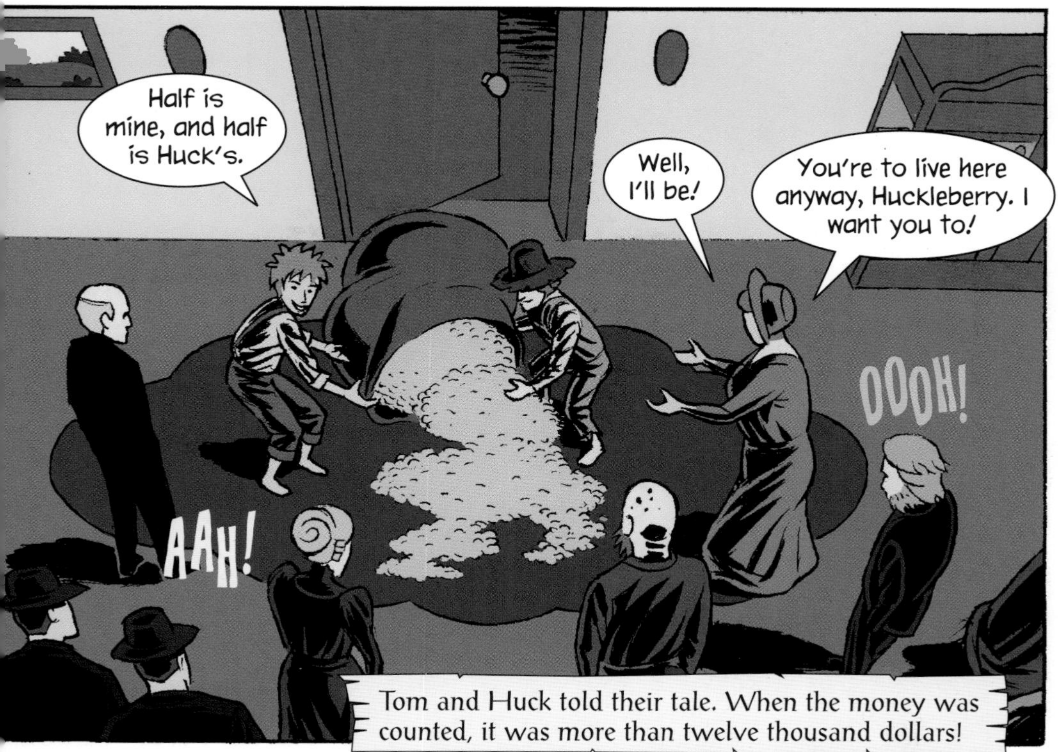
Half is mine, and half is Huck's.
Well, I'll be!
You're to live here anyway, Huckleberry. I want you to!
OOOH!
AAH!
Tom and Huck told their tale. When the money was counted, it was more than twelve thousand dollars!

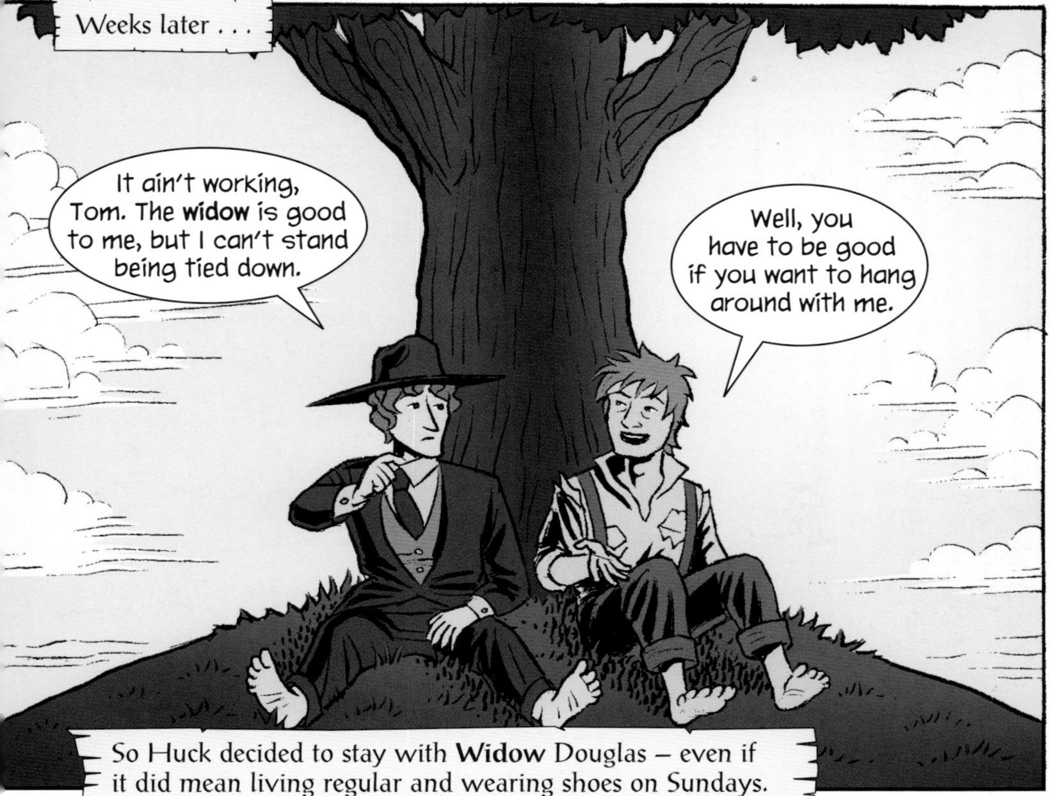
Weeks later . . .
It ain't working, Tom. The **widow** is good to me, but I can't stand being tied down.
Well, you have to be good if you want to hang around with me.
So Huck decided to stay with **Widow** Douglas — even if it did mean living regular and wearing shoes on Sundays.

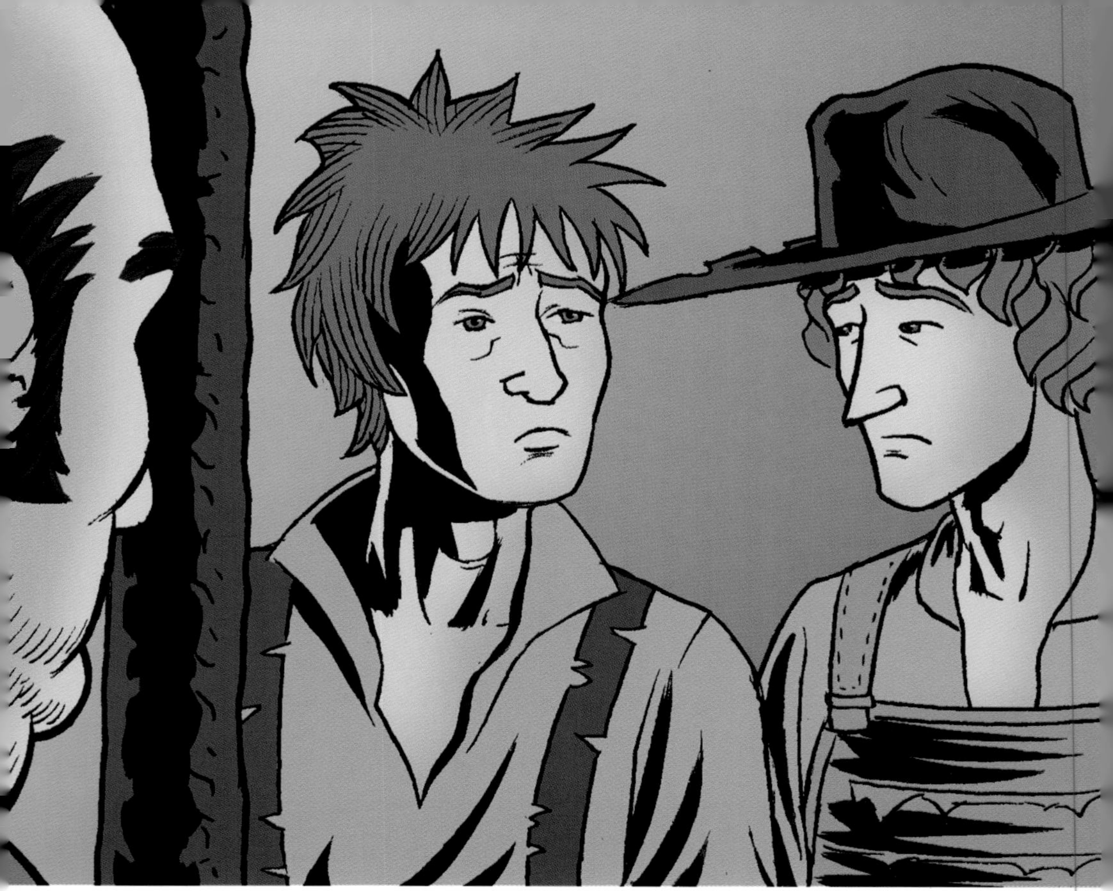

ABOUT THE RETELLING AUTHOR AND ILLUSTRATOR

M.C. Hall was born in Pennsylvania. Before becoming a writer, she worked as a classroom and reading teacher. She has written many fiction and nonfiction books for children. She enjoys reading, gardening, and walking on the beach in her free time.

Daniel Strickland has been drawing his eccentric characters ever since he could hold a pencil. He earned a degree in Sequential Art from the Savannah College of Art and Design. He creates illustrations, renders portraits, and develops original characters and stories.

GLOSSARY

cannon (KAN-un)—a big gun that sits on the ground and fires large metal balls

ferry (FARE-ee)—a boat that carries people across small bodies of water

funeral (FYOO-nuh-rul)—a ceremony held when someone dies

pirate (PYE-rit)—a person who steals from ships

punishment (PUN-ish-munt)—something you have to do or give up when you've done something wrong

starve (STARV)—die from lack of food

tannery (TAN-nur-ee)—a place where animal skins are tanned or treated to be used for leather

treasure (TREZH-ur)—money, gold, or jewels that are hidden

trial (TRY-ul)—a meeting to figure out if a person committed a crime

victim (VIK-tum)—a person who is tricked or hurt

widow (WID-oh)—a woman who didn't remarry after her husband died

COMMON CORE ALIGNED
READING QUESTIONS

1. **If you were to meet Tom in person, how might he describe himself? How would Aunt Polly describe Tom? Do you think their descriptions of Tom would be similar or different?** (*"Compare and contrast the point of view from which different stories are narrated."*)

2. **What is Tom's relationship with Becky like? How do you know? Find a few pages, quotes, and images to support your opinion.** (*"Refer to details and examples in a text when explaining what the text says explicitly and when drawing inferences from the text."*)

3. **Over the course of the story, Tom gets involved in many adventures. As a result of each of his adventures, he grows up a little and learns some valuable lessons. Can you explain how Tom's character grows throughout the course of the story? Be sure to cite certain moments in the story to support your analysis.** (*"Describe in depth a character . . . drawing on specific details in the text."*)

4. **Education and childhood play are two important themes in this story. Choose one of these two themes and write down an explanation why you think your chosen theme is more important than the other one.** (*"Determine a theme of a story."*)

5. **This adaptation of *The Adventures of Tom Sawyer* is in graphic novel format, so it uses text and illustrations to convey meaning. Find an example where the words and the illustrations work together to convey the story's meaning.** (*"Explain major differences between . . . structural elements."*)

COMMON CORE ALIGNED
WRITING QUESTIONS

1. Imagine that you used to be a part of Tom's gang, but you had to move away. What would you ask Tom about in the letters you write to him? *("Orient the reader by establishing a situation and introducing a narrator.")*

2. The young Tom Sawyer is often seen as adventurous (perhaps *too* adventurous) by the people in his town. In your opinion, do you think Tom deserves the reputation the town has given him? Or, as Tom might say, is he simply misunderstood? Write a short opinion essay taking either a person from town's perspective or Tom's point of view. *("Write opinion pieces on topics or texts, supporting a point of view with reasons and information.")*

3. Which one of Tom's adventures was your favorite, and why? Write down five reasons for your choice, making sure to use evidence (like words and images) from the graphic novel to support your choice. *("Draw evidence from literary . . . texts to support analysis.")*

4. If Tom visited you, what would he think about *your* adventures? Write a short conversation that might occur between you and Tom. *("Describe in depth a character . . . drawing on specific details in the text.")*

5. Would you recommend this graphic novel to your friends? Why or why not? Write a letter to your friends with evidence from the text to support your opinion. *("Produce clear and coherent writing in which the development and organization are appropriate to task, purpose, and audience.")*

READ THEM ALL!

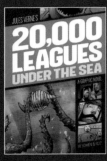

JULES VERNE'S
20,000 LEAGUES UNDER THE SEA
A GRAPHIC NOVEL
MARK TWAIN'S
THE ADVENTURES OF TOM SAWYER
A GRAPHIC NOVEL
ANNA SEWELL'S
BLACK BEAUTY
A GRAPHIC NOVEL
VICTOR HUGO'S
THE HUNCHBACK OF NOTRE DAME
A GRAPHIC NOVEL
ROBIN HOOD
A GRAPHIC NOVEL
ROBERT LOUIS STEVENSON'S
TREASURE ISLAND
A GRAPHIC NOVEL
MARY SHELLEY'S
FRANKENSTEIN
A GRAPHIC NOVEL
JULES VERNE'S
JOURNEY TO THE CENTER OF THE EARTH
A GRAPHIC NOVEL
ROBERT LOUIS STEVENSON'S
THE STRANGE CASE OF DR. JEKYLL AND MR. HYDE
A GRAPHIC NOVEL
BY BOWEN & FERRAN
WASHINGTON IRVING'S
THE LEGEND OF SLEEPY HOLLOW
A GRAPHIC NOVEL
BRAM STOKER'S
DRACULA
A GRAPHIC NOVEL
JONATHAN SWIFT'S
GULLIVER'S TRAVELS
A GRAPHIC NOVEL
ARTHUR CONAN DOYLE'S
THE HOUND OF THE BASKERVILLES
A GRAPHIC NOVEL

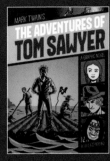

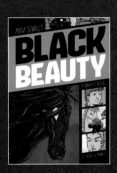

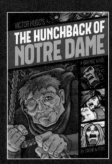

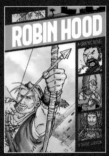

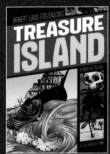

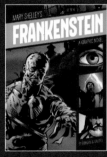

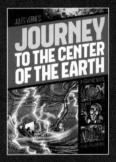

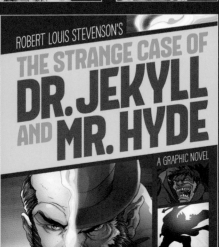

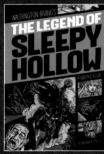

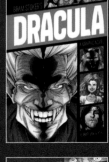

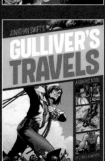

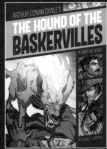

A GRAPHIC NOVEL
PERSEUS AND MEDUSA
A GRAPHIC NOVEL
LEWIS CARROLL'S
ALICE IN WONDERLAND
A GRAPHIC NOVEL
H. G. WELLS'S
THE WAR OF THE WORLDS
A GRAPHIC NOVEL
BY MILLER & BREVARD
H.G. WELLS'S
THE TIME MACHINE
A GRAPHIC NOVEL
BY DAVIS & RUIZ
KING ARTHUR AND THE KNIGHTS OF THE ROUND TABLE
A GRAPHIC NOVEL
BY HALL & RICHARDS
THE ADVENTURES OF HERCULES
A GRAPHIC NOVEL
BY POWELL & RUIZ

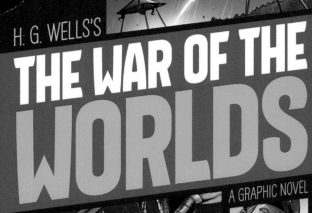

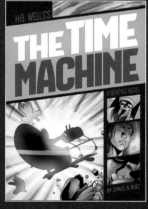

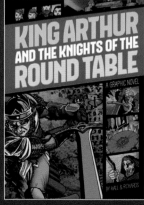

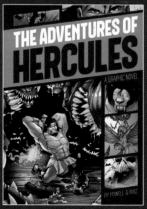